W9-BCJ-525

MISHA

A Mémoire of the Holocaust Years

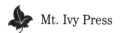

Misha Defonseca

Mt. Ivy Press

© Copyright 1997
Misha Defonseca
Mt. Ivy Press
Vera Lee

All rights reserved.

Le Chant de la Libération
© Copyright France Music 1944

Design: BECKdesign
Cover illustration: Cyrus Whittier
Cover Photo: John Nagy

Printed in U.S.A.

ISBN 0-9635257-7-8

Library of Congress
Card Catalog Number: 96-80509

Mt. Ivy Press, L.P.
Bluebell, PA

Mt. Ivy Press, Inc.
PO Box 135
Boston, MA 02258
617/244-2216

MISHA

A Mémoire of the Holocaust Years

Misha Defonseca

This book is dedicated to
the memory of Jimmy.

I love all animals on earth,
but Jimmy was my heart.

La mémoire est la source de la libération,
et l'oubli est la racine de l'exil.

BA'AL SHEM-TOV

Acknowledgments

THERE ARE MANY TO WHOM I'd like to express my gratitude: First my animals (pets and wild) who have never failed to provide me with comfort and sustenance every day of my life. I am deeply grateful for my husband Maurice and for his patient and unwavering support as I worked on this project, and for my son Morris Levy, whose presence in my life is a treasure. I am grateful for the opportunity to write this book with Vera Lee as co-author of the initial manuscript. She helped me to pour out the memories in French and then organize them in English. I offer my gratitude to Rabbi Yocheved Helligman who urged me to share my story with the congregation and my friend Janet Nirenberg who, upon hearing it, encouraged me to tell it in a book, and my publisher who heard about me by a circuitous route, searched me out and made this book a reality.

I am deeply grateful to the people of my town who have shown such kindness and understanding in my times of trouble. Thank you, thank you to Jeffrey and Sue Steele (my veteranarian); Dr. DiPaola, Sandy, Nancy and Judy; Janet and Kevin McCarron; Chris and Jim McCaffrey; Meredith and John Kilgore; Odette, John and Valerie Sullivan; Bill and Sandy Boulter; Judy and Rob Lane; Peter and Nathalie Bosse; Nancy and Bob Dills from my congregation Agudath Achim; the Garbani family, the Margolis family; Helen Rice, Ray Fridman, Bert Arling, Diane Marazzo, Pat Cunningham, Helen McLeod, The Bloomstein Family, Dave Langille, Gilmore, Inc., and the whole theatre group.

Across the ocean to Belgium I send my gratitude to: Arlette Huygh, whom I've known for 40 years, my buddy Luc Herman, Margot and Daniel; Liliane and Freddy Lehman, friends forever; Jeanine Houtekier, Andree Gillard, Andrea and Stefaan Dumery; and in Holland: the Botter family; and Eric Krauthammer in Switzerland. To these people and all others who by their actions have restored my faith in the capacity for goodness of human beings, I offer my deepest appreciation.   M.D.

THE PUBLISHER WISHES TO THANK the young scholars of Jewish culture and history, Daniella HarPaz and Susan Jacobowitz, not yet born during the time of these events, who shared their view from the next generation. To them and their children will fall the task of gleaning understanding from the ashes of the pyre; and Vera Lee for her assistance as co-author in the initial manuscript of this book. Thank you also to The Palmer & Dodge Agency for launching this book, literally, out into the whole world and Brett Kates whose loyalty and persistence is exceeded, perhaps, only by his skill. He embodies the best that the legal profession has to offer.

TABLE OF CONTENTS

International boundaries as of September 1, 1939, the day Germany invaded Poland
Courtesy: The National Geographic Magazine / Reprinted by permission.

Prologue

LOOKING BACK NOW, FROM THE COMFORT of my living room, it is hard to imagine the scale of the human devastation—the whole world at war. Who can conceive of so much death? Between 1939 and 1945, according to some historians, fifty million lives lost, six million belonged to those I called my people. Who can believe that civilization, a modern world with cars and electric lights and hospitals, could descend into the darkest madness, that hatred could roar like a firestorm across the planet?

In Europe, friend would abandon friend, neighbor would turn against neighbor, ordinary people would acquiesce by silence as their fellow citizens, men, women and even tiny babies were tortured, starved and murdered by the Nazis. Who can believe that so many could become killers without a conscience and so many, victims without a protest? Who can believe the Holocaust? And yet it happened.

I believe, because I am a witness.

No one who was alive at that time was untouched by the Second World War; many, including myself, were scarred forever. I remember as clearly as yesterday the moment the war touched my life. I was seven years old and on that day my childhood came to an end.

CHAPTER 1

Brussels
Spring, 1941

ONE PEBBLE, TWO PEBBLES, THREE PEBBLES...

I nudged the gray stones back and forth with the toe of my shoe. I studied them, pushing them into circles and squares and triangles. The other children had left long ago. The teachers were gone too.

Four pebbles, five...

I was waiting outside the big doors of my school, on the stairs that led down to the street. My father would be coming soon. He always picked me up after school. The very next time I looked up he would be coming down the street, smiling. "I couldn't get here sooner, *petite*."

The sky was getting cloudy. "If it rains I'll get wet standing here." I hugged my book to my chest. Don't move from the steps till Papa comes to get you. That was one of the important rules that I must never, ever forget.

Nine pebbles, ten pebbles...

Where was Papa? He was supposed to have come already. Where could he be?

Finally, it was not my father who came, but a woman I'd never seen before. Just a few days ago Maman had told me that might happen, that a stranger might come to meet me instead of Papa. Maman had explained that the person who picked me up would call me by name, and I was to go with her.

"Mishke?" the stranger had said. Was this unsmiling

woman in a threadbare black coat the person Maman had told me about? I nodded. Looking around nervously, she grabbed my hand and led me toward the corner without a word. I did not speak either, but my mind was racing. The woman paused to look in all directions. As she stepped off the curb, I pulled back.

"Where's Papa?"

"Shh. No questions."

The warning on her face made me understand I must not speak again. The woman's eyes darting in all directions but mine, we headed off toward my neighborhood, down the familiar path along the tram line that Papa and I always walked to and from school. As we approached my corner I could hear a commotion of some kind, a woman screaming and men's voices raised in anger. The woman in the black coat squeezed my hand and jerked my arm. "Don't look!" she hissed and pulled me forward.

I could not help looking, but all I caught was a blur: a covered truck in the middle of the street...men in uniforms. Who were those men? What was happening?

The woman tugged me forward, holding my hand so tight it hurt. The lady in the black coat said nothing. At last we reached a tram stop and the woman let go of my hand to remove some coins from a scuffed change purse. I was dying to ask her what was going on back there on my street, but she turned away and kept glancing over her shoulder and then down the street for the tram. She was in a great hurry to get away from that place.

After several minutes the yellow trolley, number 56, pulled up and stopped in front of us. It was heading for the

Gare du Midi. We climbed the tram's steep steps and the woman told me to take a seat in the back. I sat very still, staring out the window at the long rows of identical three-story brick dwellings that had been my neighborhood. Where were we going? All I could think was, "I want to go home!" Did Maman and Papa know I had been taken? Where were they? The tram jerked and bumped through the narrow, treeless streets. When the conductor came down the aisle the woman handed him some coins and he placed them in a leather pouch at his waist.

If there still was life on the other side of the window, I couldn't feel it. Images floated by me: a herring vendor with pails of salted fish dangling from his shoulders. The milk wagon loaded with shiny metal cans, parked by the curb, the milkman filling a glass bottle for a neighborhood house-wife. Bicycles, wagons, street vendors calling, mothers and fathers smiling, dogs barking and children playing—all of it surreal.

"Broukère!" The conductor boomed out the stop like a shot. A dozing businessman awoke suddenly and hurried off the tram. Two lions came into view, the stone lions that guarded the Stock Exchange. My eyes clung to them and for a moment I felt that I was in the company of strong friends.

I watched the lions until they disappeared from view as the trolley continued on its route: "La Bourse"... "Gare du Midi"... Finally we reached the terminus, a tree-lined rotary where the cars reversed direction. I picked up my school book and we got off with the last remaining passengers.

We walked on, the woman and I, still saying nothing. Now we were out of the city. I had never seen such lovely homes, so much open space. Our path led us through a park full of neatly trimmed hedges. There were trees so bedecked with blossoms that it seemed pink clouds had become ensnared in their branches. Perhaps this was the place to which I was being taken. Perhaps my parents were waiting for me in this charming spot. This certainly didn't look like a dangerous place where I could come to harm.

We passed through the park and came out the other side into an ordinary suburb of narrow streets and solid brick houses. This neighborhood still seemed more prosperous than our seedy block of row houses back in Schaerbeek, but I found it as depressing—there were no trees here and the homes all looked alike, plain and drab. Although the sidewalks were swept clean, no flowers bloomed and no children played in the doorways.

I was sinking under waves of dread when at last we turned onto a street bordered on one side by the high block wall of a factory. My guide slowed her pace and began reading aloud the numbers on each door. "Here it is," she announced as she stopped before a squat brick house. Small, tightly-curtained windows offered no clue to who or what was within. My guide reached down to take my hand again, but I pulled back. "You must come now," she said urgently. I knew at that moment, without any doubt, that there would be no use pleading, "Take me home." I accepted her outstretched hand and we walked to the front door.

I could hear the muffled buzz of the doorbell sounding in the depths of the house. As we waited outside fear tightened like a tourniquet around my chest. Suddenly the lock scraped back and the door cracked opened.

There in the dim interior stood a woman with a broad dishpan face set neckless on thick shoulders. Her precisely waved hair was pomaded flat and colored a jarringly artificial lavender shade. She took little notice of me but spoke over my head to my companion, eyeing me just once with small, close-set eyes. "Is everything taken care of?" she asked suspiciously. When my companion replied, "Yes. Everything," she motioned us to come inside. I was so terrified I could hardly move; I felt as if I had the heaviest stones in the world in my shoes.

We went down a few steps into a dimly lit room. I stopped on the last step, but the two women, ignoring me, walked to the other side of a large table and began conferring in hushed tones. Occasionally they would look in my direction as if to punctuate some point they were discussing. I heard my guide address the woman of the house as "Madame DeWael."

While the women were talking I surveyed my surroundings. We were in a dining room. As in the front, curtains at the windows were drawn tight. I studied the details: Plain whitewashed walls. On one, a gloomy landscape and on another a picture of garishly colored fruit. Even in the dim light it was easy to tell that the room was immaculate. The table top shone richly from years of careful polishing, and there was a strong smell of furniture wax and bleach in the air.

Suddenly I was jerked back to the conversation going on in the corner. "*Les parents ont été arrêtés.*" "The parents have been arrested." Whose?...my parents? For an instant, the whole room went black.

I struggled desperately to make sense of the words I'd just overheard. Papa and Maman had made sure that I was wise beyond my seven years. They had told me about the German occupation, I knew about the Gestapo. They had taught me that there was danger all around us, and I knew there were guns hidden behind the stairs in the foyer. Had I been older I might have been a bit prepared. But only at this moment did I realize, with a staggering jolt, the meaning of what I had witnessed just an hour ago on my street. *"Les parents ont été arrêtés."* My parents! With these words my heart broke.

Indifferent to my distress, the business of establishing me in a new home was proceeding efficiently. I saw my guide hand over an envelope. Madame DeWael opened it and counted the contents, cash in bills. I understood from the conversation that the money was from my parents. They must have saved up to buy my escape from the fate that might overtake them. This Madame DeWael would take me in.

"She's not an easy child," my guide confided to Madame DeWael. Did she know I could hear her? In any case the remark neither offended nor surprised me. I knew I wasn't easy. So did my parents. I felt a stab of guilt thinking about all the ways I had disobeyed them: I often fed crumbs to sparrows on the windowsill, in spite of my mother's scoldings: "How many times have I told you to stay away from the window? It's dangerous. They could see you." And I dressed up the rocking horse—a toy that a former tenant had left behind in our two-room hideout—with my own clothes. "I told you never to do that. They could come here and find you undressed." I pestered them for more food or a doll like any other girl. "We can't have those things—we're poor," my mother had explained, again and again.

The "not easy" warning didn't seem to bother Madame DeWael, who simply replied, "She'll tow the line here." Her meaning escaped me. What line was she talking about?

Before I knew what was happening, my guide was pulling her scarf over her head and saying good-bye to our hostess. I realized she was going to leave me here. As brief as our relationship, as remote as she had been with me, she was my only link to my parents. She buttoned her black coat, wished me luck without meeting my eyes and walked out the door and out of my life. I felt like the shell of an egg suddenly emptied of its contents.

Madame immediately summoned her maid, Jeannine, a fat, vulgar girl with dark hair and a florid Flemish face. "Take her up and show her to her room."

We climbed the stairs, and as we reached the second floor, Jeannine saw me staring through a doorway at an impressive collection of polished steel equipment that looked like implements of torture. "That's the doctor's office. Monsieur is a dentist," she said, with an air of importance. We continued down a dark, narrow hall and I peered into the bedrooms as we passed by each open door. Over each headboard hung a large, dark cross.

Jeannine led me to the top floor, to a space hardly bigger than a closet. It was really an extension of the landing, with no door but only a curtain separating it from the stairwell. Its furniture consisted of a narrow cot and a two-drawer dresser and its only source of light was a small square window set high in the wall. Later I would see Jeannine's room, just next to mine: large, nicely furnished, with a real door and a big, bright window.

"Madame will be up in a few minutes," she said, before heading downstairs again.

I looked up at the window and saw it was just a fixed pane with no latch or handle; there was no way of opening it. I climbed on the bed and stood there, craning my neck hard, but all I could see through the glass were gray roof gutters. I flung myself face-down on the bed and sobbed into my new pillow.

By the time I heard Madame DeWael's footsteps coming upstairs I'd had time to wipe my face and collect myself. She walked in with an armful of clothes which she placed on top of the dresser.

"You'll have to change your clothes. For your own safety, you must be unidentifiable." Then, pointing to my one piece of jewelry, a thin neck chain, she added, "And that will have to go." My hand flew to the chain. "But…"

"They could identify you with that. Here, I'll take it."

She also took possession of my book, *Blondin et Cirage*, about a white boy and his black friend. But the worst blow was seeing her take away my pencil case, my dearest possession. It was only imitation black leather but shaped like a dog, a little terrier. Finally, adding insult to injury, there were the clothes she wanted me to wear. My own clothing could hardly be called chic, but the skirts and blouses on the dresser looked so ugly to me—too elaborate, too stiff and starched.

I glanced up at Madame DeWael, trying to take the

measure of this woman I was to live with. Mirthless gray eyes stared back at me from under the pale brows.

"You'll get dressed and come downstairs. We'll be having dinner in a few minutes."

As soon as she left I was overcome by a yearning for my mother and burst into tears again. I desperately needed to feel her arms around me and hear her reassurance that everything would be all right.

From the stairway Jeannine's voice cut into my sorrow: "They're waiting for you. Are you coming down?" I sat there a while without answering, then dried my eyes and finally forced myself to get up. I examined the items of clothing on the dresser one by one, with revulsion.

Even in my state of shock at what had happened that day, I was anxious to make the best of the situation my parents had arranged for me. Choosing the least offensive skirt and blouse, I hastily pulled them on. I felt freakish wearing those strange clothes and embarrassed to be seen in them, but I had not eaten all day and the delicious smells coming up from the kitchen drew me downstairs.

In the dining room the lights were lit and the table spread with a white cloth. Madame introduced me to her dentist husband. He was a tall, blotchy-faced man with narrow, hunched shoulders. I also met their son Leopold, a camel-nosed 20-year-old, who ignored me after the introductions, the dentist and Leopold addressing all their conversation to Madame DeWael. No one could doubt for an instant that both men, as well as the maid, knew who was the head of that household.

We sat down at the table and I waited for what was in

store—a hot meal with real meat, such as we never could have dreamed of at home. I was astonished at the abundance of food brought in by Jeannine—meat and gravy, potato dumplings and honeyed carrots, cabbage with a rich cream sauce and fresh bread with a crock of butter.

Graced with this feast, everyone seemed to relax, even Madame DeWael. The dentist, I discovered on that occasion, had the peculiar habit at mealtime of humming the same word over and over to himself in different tones. Leopold and Madame seemed not to notice as they chatted and smiled, and soon I was smiling too. That is, until the dentist got on his wife's nerves by humming too loudly, "Bonjour, bonjour, bonjour..." on every note of the scale.

"Must you do that?"

"Sorry, Marguerite." But he soon started up again.

Later, seeing me scooping up every last morsel of meat with a piece of bread, Madame DeWael asked, "Do you know what kind of meat that is?"

"No."

"Do you like it?"

"Yes, it's delicious."

"It's bacon." She laughed, revealing a mouthful of gold teeth I hadn't noticed before, and I wondered if they were a present from Monsieur DeWael. Her son was laughing with her, and Jeannine, serving from a platter, joined in the merriment, so I obligingly laughed along with them. It wasn't until much later that I understood they were laughing at me, a Jewish child for whom bacon should have been an unthinkable food.

The next morning, on the way down to breakfast, I overheard Jeannine telling Madame DeWael, "I couldn't sleep a wink all night, she was crying so loud." Madame frowned at me when I entered the dining room.

Once again the table was spread with a clean white cloth and set with places for the DeWael family and me. I slid into the seat I had occupied the night before, wondering if last night's feast would be repeated. It was. Fat golden loaves of Belgian bread and a jar full to the lip with ruby red strawberry preserves sat across the table. Leopold informed me proudly that his mother did all the cooking for the household. I was impressed. Whatever her other failings, Madame DeWael could certainly do one thing right.

The dentist cut a thick slice of bread and placed it on my plate. My mouth was watering as I waited for Leopold to pass the strawberry jam. My family never had such a wonderful treat. When the jam came my way I helped myself to a heaping spoonful and spread it over my bread. Just as I was about to take a bite, the bread was abruptly snatched from my hand by Madame DeWael.

"Will you look at that!" she said, displaying it to her son and the dentist. "Look at the piggy amount of preserves she took! Did you ever see such a thing? She'll ruin us!" She took her knife and proceeded to scrape almost all the jam back into the jar, then returned the slice of bread to me with only the faintest trace of pink.

Did the others laugh? I don't remember. But neither do I recall a look of compassion from anyone there. As for

Madame DeWael, the woman offended me in many, more serious ways during my time there, but that little act of hers still stands out in my memory.

After breakfast I remained alone with Madame DeWael. Targeting me with those little gray eyes, she proceeded to list her immediate plans for me, ticking off each item with cool efficiency.

"We'll have your photograph taken with your new identity. First we must do something about that hair. The bangs will have to be pulled back. In fact, all your hair should be swept back, like mine—much more chic in any case. Your name will be changed. We'll call you Monique. Not that nickname—what is it?"

"Mishke."

"Yes, no more of that. Sounds Jewish. And you'll call me 'Maman.'"

Each directive felt like a punch in the stomach. I would have to submit to the new hairdo and the change of name— but call her "Maman"? She was not my mother! Had she asked me to call her by her first name, Marguerite, I could have managed that, but even for safety's sake, never, never "Maman."

She finished her catalog of things to do with a list of rules and regulations for me: I must not open the closets. I must not help myself to food from the kitchen, but eat only what was served at meals. Since it was too dangerous for me to go to school, I'd be home a lot, but I must not sit around idly. She expected me to pitch in, helping with the housework or assisting her with her sewing. Several times a week I would walk the few kilometers to Grandfather's farm and bring back eggs, vegetables, milk and whatever else she needed. ("Grandfather," it turned out, was what everyone called Monsieur DeWael's uncle.)

We went out that afternoon and I had my picture taken in one of those "Polyphoto" shops where pictures were developed while you waited. My hair style was changed and I was wearing the new clothes Madame had chosen for me. I had a peek at the picture and could barely recognize myself. On the back of my photo was my new name: "Monique DeWael." I was given a date of birth making me only four years old, but because I was so small for my age and looked so young, no one would have suspected that anything was amiss.

I managed to get through the day without addressing Madame DeWael as either "Maman" or "Madame," though I knew it was rude for a little girl to say "yes," "no," or "thank you" to a lady without adding her name or title.

At the end of the week Leopold walked me to Grandfather's farm so I'd know the way when I went to pick up the produce. It was a pleasant hike through fields and meadows. I would have loved to dawdle, to stay there all by myself, the spring sunlight warming my hair, drinking in the rich and acrid smells of hay and loam and fresh manure. Perhaps I could do that when I made the trip on my own.

As we stood on the porch of the sprawling white farmhouse we could hear some sort of machine chunk-chunking away.

"That's Marthe and her sewing machine." Leopold said.
"Marthe?"

"Grandfather's wife. She's always sewing. She can sew just about everything. She used to be a milliner."

We walked around to the back of the house. There stood Grandfather, waist deep in the pea patch, examining the little green pods for readiness. As we approached, he slowly unbent his big frame and eyed me closely as if to size me up. I stood still and did the same to him. He had a mane of white hair, a thick white mustache and an impressive amber pipe that was clenched firmly in his teeth. He wore an open shirt with a stand-up officer's collar, wide peasant trousers and wooden shoes.

He glanced coolly at Leopold and uttered an unsmiling, "Come in." We followed him into the kitchen. An airy room with a stone floor, it was dominated by a huge cast iron wood stove with two oven doors, four burners and damp dish towels hanging to dry from a thin chrome rail around the edge.

Grandfather's wife nodded at us from her sewing machine in the corner, then slowly stood up, smoothing down the white apron that ran the length of her long cotton skirt. She was a tall, portly woman with a generous bosom, a pleasant, though serious, face and graying chestnut hair drawn back into a chignon.

"I'd like you to meet Monique." Leopold formally introduced me to both of them and I beamed my most ingratiating smile. Grandfather nodded without returning my smile and motioned us to sit. Leopold pulled a wooden armchair to the kitchen table and handed Grandfather a small brown packet. I gathered that it contained something relating to me but couldn't figure out what it was. Too flat to hold my dog pencil case—perhaps it was my chain, sent to the farm for safekeeping? I wouldn't find out what was in that envelope until much later, after the end of the war.

Grandfather did not open the envelope but instead set it under the salt cellar in the middle of the table. There was an awkward pause. We sat in silence until suddenly, out of nowhere, Grandfather announced that he would show me around. Leopold got up to accompany us, but the old man pointed his finger at the boy, fixed him with a stern look and snapped, "You stay there." Awed by this performance, I followed him meekly out the back door.

The big man grabbed his cane from its peg outside and set off down the path, pointing out the features of interest as he went. "This is the herb garden where Marthe grows woodruff and chamomile and thyme and the like. The hives are close by," he said waving his cane in the direction of some white boxes on stilts, "so the bees can visit the herb flowers. That's why their honey tastes so good." The path wound along a row of cherry trees that had almost finished blooming. Their white petals lay on the ground like petticoats around their ankles.

Grandfather's tour continued along strawberry beds neatly mulched with hay and through a grove of gnarled apple trees. As we passed the stone dairy barn Grandfather promised to show me around inside on my next visit. We stopped at the pig sty where a huge white sow lay in mud with a row of pink piglets nuzzling at her belly, then strolled past a flock of speckled guinea fowl pecking for beetles at the side of the road.

On a hill overlooking newly tilled fields just beginning to show traces of green, like whiskers on a teenager's chin, Grandfather invited me to sit down with him. He leaned back against the trunk of an old magnolia tree in extravagant bloom, its sweet-sharp perfume clinging to our every breath. I reached up, picked a blossom and began to examine it, waiting. Each thick petal was as pink and soft as a dog's tongue.

Finally he spoke to me about me: "So you're going to come to get the eggs?"

"Yes."

He puffed on his pipe a while.

"You're not going to break them, are you?"

"No...I mean I'll try not to."

He fell silent for a moment and examined my face.

"Do you want to see the hens?"

I looked up. Was that a hint of friendliness in his eyes?

"Yes!" I nearly yelled the word.

He burst out laughing. Then he led me back to the barnyard and we came to a coop of noisy, bustling hens and chicks wandering in and out of the little doorway. In the midst of the flock strutted a handsome bird with white speckles spattered over iridescent black feathers. She was without doubt the most enchanting creature in the barnyard and I couldn't take my eyes away from her.

"That's our 'coucou de Malines.' It's a type of hen that comes from the Malines region. Do you want to pick her up?"

"I can pick her up?" I couldn't believe my luck. Quietly tip-toeing over to the hen, I managed, after two or three tries, to gather her in my arms, but she quickly skittered away. Grandfather smiled reassuringly. "Never mind, you can try again next time, *petite*."

"*Petite*." He had called me by the pet name my parents always used! And he was going to let me pick up the *coucou de Malines* next time. And I'd be coming back there regularly for the DeWaels' supplies—not with Leopold but all by myself. For the first time since my parents' disappearance I forgot the hole deep in my chest— and the pain of living under the same roof with Marguerite DeWael.

Back at the house Madame DeWael was putting away the milk, butter, spinach and lettuce we'd carried back.

"What did he say?" I heard her ask Leopold.

"Same as usual."

Then she turned to me: "And you'll know how to get there on your own?"

"Yes, it's easy. And I can carry everything back by myself. And Grandfather showed me the hens. He let me pick up the *coucou de Malines*! And he said I could be in charge of putting the chickens back in the coop, and..."

"Young lady," she cut in, "If you waste time fooling around there, we'll never get our dinner back in time. I'm entrusting you with this important chore, do you understand? This is not a game."

"I understand." I understood only that I had to be careful, on guard, and not blurt out the first thing that came into my head.

That night I cried again for Maman and Papa. The loneliness was far worse after my visit to the farm. I remembered lying between my parents in bed in our little flat,
getting to sleep by caressing Maman's earlobe, my lips
moving constantly, as though sucking a lollipop. When her
earlobe got too warm, Maman let me use her cool one, until
Papa, with exasperation would say, "But really! Is she going
to do that when she's married?"

Much later, recalling his words, I thought, how amazing: Even with the danger surrounding Jews in this war,
they still assumed I would survive to get married, to live a
"normal" life.

I could not fall asleep. My stomach was growling from
hunger. In fact, I would always be hungry at the DeWaels';
although Madame's meals were finer than anything I'd been
used to back in Schaerbeek, she put so many restrictions
on what and when I could eat, I never had enough. She had
declared the larder and ice box off limits, but now lying
there in the dark I began to wonder: Could I perhaps sneak
down after everyone was asleep? I sat up in bed and listened intently. I could just make out muffled voices below. I
got up, pushed aside the curtain separating my room from
the landing and stood at the top of the stairs.

The stairs ended on the floor below directly outside
Madame DeWael's bedroom. I could see light spilling through
her open door onto the striped hall rug. I went down several
steps, avoiding the third one that creaked, and sat there listening. Yes, they were still up, in her room, talking. Madame's
voice went on and on, with an occasional word or two from
Leopold. She was complaining about Grandfather. I heard her

say, "The man is infuriating!" and could picture the way her lips got thinner when she was displeased.

After a while I heard Leopold bid her good-night and go to his room. Finally all was quiet. In my bare feet I walked as gingerly as possible down the stairs, directly to the kitchen. The house was dark as a cave. By decree of the Germans, as in every other home in the village, on every window we had dark blue shades whose purpose it was to block the lamplight so Allied bombers could not find their targets.

Even in the dark I went straight to the cupboard that contained the painted tin biscuit can that served as a cookie jar. The door protested with a tiny squeak as I opened it. I waited a moment then lifted out the can, pried off the lid and reached my hand inside. Ah, success: *"Spéculoos"*— the brown sugar cookies that Madame had baked earlier that day! I moved across the room, gently opened the tin-lined wooden ice box in the corner and carefully removed the milk. In one hand, a fistful of cookies, in the other, a pitcher of creamy milk from the farm—I devoured three cookies at once and washed them down with big gulps right out of the pitcher.

Was that a noise? Someone was coming downstairs! I slid behind the door as the footsteps came nearer. Peeking out the crack between the door hinges, I saw it was Leopold on his way to the bathroom. As soon he was out of sight I returned my purloined bounty to where I'd found it and flew upstairs to bed.

The next morning Madame had words for me: Hadn't she told me not to help myself to food in the kitchen? Was

I too stupid to understand simple rules? Why was I so rebellious? Seeing the way Leopold turned his eyes away throughout the lecture, I had no doubt about who had snitched on me.

Before she finished with me she announced, "Today is Jeannine's day off. I'll expect you to help with the cleaning."

I hated those chores. Not that they were difficult or repellent in themselves. But washing, mopping or scrubbing up while La DeWael tended to her business always made me feel like a servant. No, not a servant, a slave. I was worse off than a servant since the maid had better sleeping quarters than I did, and she was never scolded but treated with respect.

Afterwards, I spent a couple of hours in the top floor sewing room with Madame DeWael. She was at her machine just under the skylight, while I sat on cushions against the wall, winding bobbins of thread and basting pattern pieces. She began grilling me about Grandfather: Did he ask about her family? Did he say anything in particular? Remembering her criticism of the old man and her displeasure that I had enjoyed our time in the barnyard, I thought it wiser not to give her any specifics. She wasn't satisfied with that and she certainly wasn't satisfied with me.

"Are you sewing there or dreaming? And is that how I told you to baste? Can't you ever go in a straight line? Why is it I am always disappointed with you?"

For the remainder of that afternoon I was completely silent, while Madame addressed a running monologue about nothing of importance to no one in particular.

The days grew longer and summer arrived. At night, I lay awake for hours waiting for my stuffy little space at the top of the stairs to surrender the heat of the day. My loneliness and I often kept watch in the darkness long after the house fell silent. I lay still, looking out at the distant stars framed in the tiny window above my bed. Although I was by now beyond crying, the loss of my parents was a throbbing wound. I knew just where it was and could explore it, touching it in my mind the way my mother would press gently on a hidden splinter and ask, "Is this where it hurts?"

Nights were hard, but each long summer day in the DeWael's home was its own eternity. There was never a waking moment in that dark house when I did not feel the blade in my heart. I had a roof over my head but I was without a home. I was an outsider, an outlaw, always on guard, always having to lie and pretend.

Several times a week I trekked to the farm for supplies. The walk took about three quarters of an hour, and even in rainy weather, I felt free as I daydreamed my way along with an empty milk jug dangling from my hand, a knapsack slung over my shoulder. My journey took me past pastures grazed by sweet-faced cows and through fields of corn and wheat and rye patrolled by flocks of argumentative crows. When I came to a pond I would stop to see if there were any new arrivals—fuzzy little ducklings from the pond's domestic residents, or wild geese, pausing to feed along their ancient migratory routes.

With the passing of time I had come to know Grandfather and Marthe better and to trust them both. The hours I spent with them were the only times I knew any happiness. And I came to feel that I was an important part of their lives too. At first I wasn't sure about Marthe. She was sometimes quiet and withdrawn, not joining in with Grandfather and me when we were playing a game or talking about some interesting matter. Grandfather explained to me that she had moments of grief because of the death of their only son. I never learned exactly how and when he died.

Perhaps in some way having a child like me around was a consolation. Sometimes, without realizing it, she called me "Joseph," her dead son's name, but I always answered her without correcting the mistake.

Marthe worried about some of my tomboy capers around the farm. In spite, or perhaps because, of an acute fear of heights, I loved to climb to the highest beam of the hayloft and jump into the sweet smelling hay below, then repeat my brave feat again and again. When Marthe saw me do it she feared for my life and pleaded with Grandfather to make me stop. He just told her, "Let her do it; it's good for her." So she said nothing more. But by the time of my next visit she had sewn me a floral skirt with wide bloomers that matched, so I could do my climbing and jumping comfortably and decently. She enjoyed doing things like that for me.

Marthe made me other play clothes, pants and shirts mostly, so that I could run around and play without worrying about soiling or ripping Madame's fussy dresses. I loved those clothes and all the freedom they gave me, but Madame felt otherwise. When I returned home one day wearing a pair of Marthe's play pants, she was furious: "You look like a tough boy in those things. Here I've been doing my best to get you to be more ladylike, and she puts you into that get-up!" Then, to my horror, she confiscated the pants.

When I told Marthe what had happened, she was sitting at the kitchen table, her fingers and nails black from the walnuts she was shucking to sell at market that week. She simply said, "Never mind, I'll make you more and we'll keep them here for you."

Grandfather was definitely not fond of Madame. He told me he once had ordered her out of his house, and after that she never came to visit him again. In order to get fresh produce to supplement the meager wartime rations, she had her son—and now me—make the trip. The old man obliged; these folks were, after all, his nephew's family.

Two people couldn't be more dissimilar than Ernest DeWael and Marguerite DeWael. Even the ways they showed their dislike for each other were different. She regarded him with open hostility and spoke of him in a tone of seething resentment. He simply dismissed her as unworthy of the effort it would take to despise her. Though at times he might call her "the witch" or "the money-grubbing harpy," most of the time he referred to her humorously. For instance, once, when we were speaking about good-looking women, he said,

"Now look at that pint-sized Marguerite. You never hear people say 'So-and-so is a short, beautiful, figure of a woman.' They say…" And here Grandfather proudly pointed his pipe in Marthe's direction…"They say, 'So-and-so is a *tall*, beautiful figure of a woman!'"

The old man was aware that Madame pumped me for

information each time I returned from the farm. When I came to feel comfortable with both of them, I treated them to an imitation of La DeWael greeting me as I walked in the door, her arms folded at her bosom: "So? What did he say?"

In the beginning I'd been foolish enough to let her see my pleasure in the farm visits and had revealed too much for my own good. Armed with that information, when she needed to punish me for something, she sent Leopold to the farm and made me stay with her doing chores. Grandfather's advice was: "Don't tell anyone anything, *petite*. People will use what you say to hurt you."

Proud that I had learned the lesson, a few weeks later when I gave him my imitation of Madame grilling me, the lines went:

La DeWael: "So? What did he say?"

Me (innocently): "Grandfather? Oh, he said to be sure to send you his best regards."

La DeWael (tight-lipped): "I'm sure of that!"

Grandfather chuckled hearing the dialogue and commented approvingly, "You're getting to be a devil."

But later, speaking seriously with him, I told him what had begun to bother me more and more.

"I'm getting to be bad, Grandfather. I think she's making me into a bad girl, lying and being sneaky all the time, so she won't get mad at me."

The old man looked at me sadly for a moment, then he said, "No, petite, you won't turn bad, because deep in your heart you are good."

As reassuring as his words were, they didn't completely convince me. I knew that living with Madame DeWael was turning me into something I didn't want to be.

Still, my world did have a just and righteous center and it was Grandfather. Being with him several times a week almost canceled out all the indignities and humiliations I endured at the hands of Madame DeWael. How many favors did he do for me? How many surprises did he plan? One time it was a swing he'd made and suspended from a big walnut tree. Another day he presented me with a gift wrapped in a bit of paper and tied with string, the first gift I ever received.

It was a little leather billfold with compartments where I could put all my treasures: a pretty leaf, a feather shed by the *coucou de Malines*; anything precious, anything with meaning might be stored away in it. "Grandfather gave this to me and it's mine," I thought. Somehow I had to identify it as my own, but I couldn't very well engrave my name on it. Instead, I bit hard into one corner of the billfold, and to my delight the teeth marks proved indelibly that this gift was mine alone.

Too good to be true. One day, back in my bedroom, I discovered my treasure had disappeared. I emptied my drawers and tore off my bedclothes looking for it, to no avail. Frantic, I ran to Jeannine's room to ask her if she'd seen it. Before she had time to answer, I spotted it lying right there on her bed.

"My wallet!" I cried, grabbing it eagerly.

"What do you mean—it's mine," she replied.

I stood there dumbfounded for a moment, anger and outrage welling up in me. Then I ran downstairs and told Madame the whole story. Meanwhile Jeannine had followed me down. She calmly assured her mistress that the object belonged to her.

"But look—I bit into it. Here are my teeth marks."

As Madame DeWael examined the imprint, Jeannine explained, "No, the teeth marks are mine."

"Yes, of course this is Jeannine's billfold. After all, where would Monique get such a thing?"

I couldn't, wouldn't tell her it was a present from Grandfather, possibly jeopardizing my visits to the farm. And it would have been useless to submit the teeth marks to the dentist himself; he never would have taken my part against his formidable wife. I finally understood the case was already decided and I had lost.

"It's all right, *petite*," Grandfather said, when I told him about the billfold. "I'll get you something else."

Could I have survived without the farm? I don't know. After the stifling atmosphere of Madame's house, it was light, breath and sustenance. Images and impressions of those visits would remain with me forever: Grandfather milking the cows and letting me drink right from the pail. Grandfather reaching high up into the peach tree to pick me a ripe pink peach and smiling as the juice ran down my arms and chin.

I also remember Marthe in a playful mood, dressing me like a princess in scarves, shawls and long skirts and making up my eyes with liner and mascara. (Some black remained on my lids and lashes after I got home, much to Madame's horror: "She wants to make you into a tramp!")

I remember so clearly the two black and white Spaniels, "Ita" and "Rita"—each with black spots on their ears. When I arrived at the farm they always greeted me by putting their front paws on my chest and licking my face, then rolling on their backs and wiggling. I hugged and kissed them back and fell to the ground and the three of us rolled and tumbled about with total abandon, as if the world really was a safe place after all.

In the room where Grandfather and Marthe slept there was a picture I loved to gaze at: beautiful ladies ensconced in a long boat traveling down a stream in the woods. They were clad in gauzy shawls of every color—rose, azure, mauve, amber—silky veils billowing in the wind. Grandfather explained they were "nymphs of the forest," and though I didn't quite understand the concept of nymphs, I wanted to look just like them when I grew up.

And I remember Grandfather's maps. He would spread them out on the big kitchen table and we spent many hours studying them together. I was fascinated by those charts. Grandfather would point out the continents, the oceans, the mountains and dense forests. "Here is where we are, in Belgium. These red lines are the borders of countries and the blue lines are the rivers." He would point to the map and ask me to read the names of all the different places.

My heart swelled with pride when the old man noticed how fast I learned. Unlike Madame, Grandfather often gave me compliments. He would tell me, "You have a very keen memory," and "Hey, you're a darned good reader!" Later, looking back on those times, I would see them as an education in geography a thousand times more valuable than lessons any school could have offered me.

I especially remember Grandfather showing me the map of Germany where he'd spent time before the war. There he'd learned strange words like "*kartoffeln*," meaning potatoes. Of course that was Germany before the war, but now Germany was the home of those filthy *boches* who at this moment were invaders in our country.

"The *boches* took my mother and father, didn't they? Are they in Germany now?"

"Perhaps…"

"So how could one get to Germany?"

"Why it's east of Belgium, see? Here's where we are, in Belgium, then there's the Ardennes, then east of that is Germany and there's the Rhine," he explained, tracing the route with the stem of his pipe.

Then he was reminded of something. "Ah, I promised you something to replace the billfold, right? Wait there."

He came back with a tiny, white cowry shell, no bigger than a tooth. In fact it looked just like a molar to me, with a circular window, smaller than a collar button, set in the middle.

"What is it?"

"It's a compass. Like my big one, remember? It tells the direction you're going in, so you won't get lost. See—the little blue needle is pointing to N. That means north."

"A compass!" I examined it with delight, rolled it around lovingly in my hand, then looked again at the tiny face with the arrow.

"But suppose I want to visit my parents in Germany. Didn't you say that was east?"

"Of course. East is right here to the right." And he

added: "Now don't let the harpy find this one. Perhaps you should leave it and use it here."

I agreed to leave it at the farm most of the time and to be very, very careful if it ever came home with me.

That night at the dinner table the conversation turned to the bridge near the oil depot that had been bombed out. That day Leopold and the baker's son had walked the several miles to the site to see if it was being rebuilt. It wasn't, he reported.

There followed a tense discussion: Was it just the Jews who were in danger? What about the rest? What demands would the filthy Germans make on Belgians? All the Jews had been ordered to register, but everyone knew there were plenty of them who had no intention of putting their names on any German list. "They ought to cooperate so they don't get the rest of us in trouble," pronounced Madame.

While the discussion continued, my eyes never left the napkin I clutched tightly in my lap. I could not eat my dinner though it was many hours since my last meal.

For me, Grandfather was as solid and strong as an oak tree. It was he who could protect me from the danger I knew surrounded me. But more important, he could teach me how to be strong. Once, when I offered to help him bring in wood for the stove, he pointed to a big log and asked me to carry it to him. When I hesitated, not sure I could lift it by myself, he said, "You're stronger than you think. Just try and you'll see."

I did try to raise the log, pulling and straining with

enormous effort. After dropping it twice, at last I managed to hoist it onto one shoulder. Proud of my accomplishment I drew myself up as tall as I could and beamed at Grandfather. Athos of *The Three Musketeers* (who would later become my favorite fictional hero) couldn't have been more pleased with himself after his finest victory.

I wanted to be as forceful and unshakable as Grandfather—not an easy goal for such a little girl. Still I always had his example before me.

One instance at the farm I'll never forget, when planes came buzzing overhead. They sounded so close, Marthe and I were frightened out of our wits. There had been bombings at several strategic sites in the area. For safety's sake there was now a curfew. Everyone had to stay home at night. And the sight of a squadron of German planes raking the sky on their way to bomb French or British targets, or the reverse, wasn't unusual.

But that afternoon at the farm the war planes overhead were so loud that Marthe, her sweet face frozen and white, grabbed my hand and began to run.

"Come, to the cellar—quickly!" Her fear was contagious and I too ran for safety.

"No!" Grandfather's voice stopped us in our tracks. "No!" he shouted above the roar of the planes. Then, gently but firmly, he said to us, "Come out here a minute," and headed for the door.

After some hesitation, Marthe released my hand. Still fearful, she slowly followed him outdoors, while I, figuring that Grandfather must be right as usual, went with her.

"Here," he said, planting his feet firmly on the ground.

"If they're going to get me they can get me right here. If I'm going to die it won't be down in the cellar like a frightened rat." Then he raised his clenched fists to the sky. "I'll do it here, in the open, you see?"

From the beginning, each visit to the farm was followed by waves of loneliness and longing for my parents. The return to the DeWaels' house never failed to plunge me into the darkest gloom. Even before walking in, I felt a knot in my stomach and my whole body tensed up. I knew as soon as I opened the door the endless litany of belittling and disapproval would commence.

Grandfather could see how miserable I was and how much I dreaded going back to there. Once, just as we were saying good-bye, he gave me some helpful advice:

"Don't let her know your feelings. Smile at her. Play a little game with her. For example, next time you get back late pick her some flowers to distract her from scolding you."

The advice paid off, at least in the short term. One afternoon, I dawdled a little too long on the way home, stopping to play with a wild barn cat from a neighbor's farm. Back on the path I quickly gathered a few wildflowers, and as I walked in the door handed the bouquet to Madame. "Here—I picked these for you."

Her pursed lips relaxed into a faint smile and she said "Thank you" and didn't bother me the rest of the day. Later I heard her tell a friend, almost boastfully, about my gift.

The only gift she ever gave me was unintentional, but

wonderful nevertheless. She and her family had to go some-
where for several days and I was to stay at the farm. When
I told Grandfather, he said to Marthe, "This will give you
two a chance to get out of the house and have some fun.
Why don't you ladies go into town Saturday afternoon?
Have some lunch, do a little shopping."

Into town! That could only mean the big city: Brussels.
How could I wait until then?

It was a brisk day in early September. Marthe had made
me a little hat that perched coquettishly like a sparrow over
my forehead, and we both wore new dresses and smart
coats. I had never seen Marthe looking so chic, but that was
as it should be because we were going into the city.

We went there by tram, all the way to a beautiful
square, La Grande Place. I marveled at the graceful public
buildings, ornamented with all manner of turrets, arches,
fancy grillwork, bay windows and balconies, and at the ele-
gant shops and all the people parading in and out of
them—especially the women with their charming hats,
smart suits and high heels. The sidewalks were full of people sitting at café tables under big umbrellas. And I'd never
seen so many cars in one place.

Marthe took me to a corner café with a red awning
where she treated me to a glass of milk and a buttery,
mocha cream pastry, and herself to a cup of tea. As much
as I was a tomboy at the farm, here I felt like a young lady.

Then Marthe gave me a great surprise. We walked into
a shop "just to look" and came out with a doll, a doll like

some girls at school in Schaerbeek had, but this one would be my very own, and, in my opinion, a thousand times more beautiful. She had a delicate face with rosy cheeks and a dress decorated with white lace. She was the first doll I ever owned.

When it was time to go back, we boarded the tram again, I clutching my doll for dear life. Then, at our stop, as we stepped off the tram a German soldier began to board, and his bayonet suddenly caught in my doll, ripping the lace of her dress. I couldn't believe it. Horrified, I shouted the first thing that came into my head—Grandfather's phrase about the filthy Germans.

"*Sale boche! Sale boche!*" I yelled at him at the top of my lungs. The soldier ignored me, while Marthe anxiously shushed me and pulled me away by the hand as fast as she could.

But even the violation of my doll couldn't spoil that special weekend. I remember how, as it grew dark that night, I sat outside on a bench next to Grandfather watching the big harvest moon rise over the horizon. The evening was so peaceful, with only the ceaseless chirping of crickets and the rhythmic little salutations of frogs to break the stillness. A soft breeze played over my face as I raised my head. The sky was curtain of deep blue velvet on which the moon was suspended like a great silver platter. Suddenly I felt an intense yearning.

"Grandfather—I want the moon."

He looked at me a moment but with no trace of surprise.

"You want the moon, *petite*? Wait..." He raised both hands high and appeared to seize the gleaming orb, pulling it down and offering it to me with great formality. "Here. Here you have the moon."

I pretended to cradle it in my arms, rocking it back and forth contentedly for a while and then said "Grandfather—I want another one."

The old man roared with laughter and I joined in.

For the next several weeks I managed to get along with Madame by following Grandfather's advice. I played the game, obeying her like a good girl, trying to be cheerful and doing nothing that might offend her. I continued to hide my pleasure in the farm visits and kept quiet about anything Grandfather said. But now I also went out of my way to flatter her with little compliments and I even invented tidbits of news to fill up pauses in the conversation. One thing I could not do, however, was call her "Maman." That angered her to no end, but I simply could not.

Despite my latest and best efforts, the threads by which our tenuous relationship held together ultimately snapped. One night, as I sat eavesdropping on the stairs, I heard Madame confide to a friend,

"If my maid were to leave me, I'd shed bitter tears. But if that girl went—good riddance!"

I had been trying so hard to be what she wanted me to be; I felt as though she'd slapped me in the face. That remark was nothing compared to what I heard several nights later.

"Oh we'll keep her, of course. If the Allies win the war, we'll get points for saving a Jew. And if the Germans win, we'll get in good with them by handing her over."

From that time on there was no question of playing a game with her, of pretending to be sweet and dutiful. I sat facing her in stony silence as I wound her bobbins. But my sense of betrayal was so profound there was no way to hide it. When I clenched my teeth and refused to speak at all, Madame taunted me.

"You say nothing. You just sit there with your mouth shut, but I can see the insolence in your eyes."

I had taken to keeping the tiny compass with me at all times, hiding it sometimes in a pocket. Now, in the sewing sessions with Madame, I often held it inside one cheek—an added inducement to keep my mouth closed in her company.

One time, however, I could not stay mute. She was berating me once more for not calling her "Maman."

"When I think of what I've done for you... How many people would have done so much? I've done more for you than your own mother."

"No."

"No! What do you mean, no?"

"She gave me my life."

"Oh, fine, she gave you your life. And where is she now?"

How could she say a thing like that? How could anybody even think that? My heart nearly burst with a hatred such as I'd never felt in my life.

At that moment I knew I had to get out. There was no way I could stay in that house, near that woman, any longer. Instead, I yearned to be with my mother and father. There had to be some way to find them. I had to escape. Escape soon. But how?

When the anger subsided I began to make plans. At night I'd lie in bed and scheme. Winter would be coming soon, so I would wear my heaviest clothes when I left. I'd take sturdy play pants from the farm to Madame's house, smuggling them there under my jacket... and that wonderful wool cap Marthe had knitted for me, the navy blue one with multi-colored thin stripes. It extended into a long tasseled "tail" I could wear around my neck as a scarf. All the better that with my pants on and my hair covered by the cap, no one would recognize me as a girl.

There was just one problem: The only pair of shoes that fit me were the pumps La DeWael had me wear, and they looked nothing like boys' shoes. Oh, well, the pants were long and would cover them.

On the next trip I took some clothes from the farm and hid them under my mattress. Would Marthe notice they were gone? I hadn't thought that far ahead. As I lay in bed that night I went over the list of important items to take next and planned my getaway.

The following weekend was the last time I ever saw the farm. I had just arrived when Grandfather took me aside and said, "*Petite*, you can't come here any more. It's too dangerous. They have been here asking questions..."

I nodded but couldn't speak a word. This one piece of solid ground had dissolved into quicksand under my feet; I was falling off a precipice into a deep and endless hole. Before I left the farm that day I gathered the rest of my necessary items and smuggled them home.

My plans and preparations continued over the next week. Next to the warm play clothes from the farm, now carefully hidden under my mattress, I tucked the tiny compass. As Grandfather had shown me, it wasn't just a toy and it really could tell where east was. I was certain it could guide me to my parents in Germany. I also examined the knives Madame kept in a drawer in the kitchen and selected a short sturdy one, then put it back and closed the drawer. It would be ready when the time came.

Each night I went over the details. At the last moment I would take the knapsack for carrying eggs and vegetables and hide it under the mattress, along with a length of twine for carrying bread. I would know in advance exactly what food I could snitch from the kitchen. The timing had to be right, not in the daytime, even if everyone were out of the house, but some night when Jeannine had the weekend off and the others were all asleep. And I must follow the route with the fewest houses—toward the canal and the woods beyond.

Planning my escape I had no fear, no thought of the dangers out there, only an overwhelming urge to get away and find my parents as soon as possible.

Several nights later I again lay in bed wide-eyed and rigidly alert while the rest of the household was fast asleep. Through the tiny window over my bed I could see the moon, round and full, without a cloud to dim its brightness. Now. Now is the time. I slid out of bed and pulled my stash from under the mattress. In the tiny patch of moonlight coming through my window I dressed myself in Marthe's play clothes, a heavy sweater and my navy blue quilted jacket. Then, with a pair of scissors I'd taken from the kitchen cabinet, I began cutting my hair every which way, clipping it as close as possible to my scalp. I didn't care how messy it was so long as I didn't look like somebody's little girl.

I pushed the little compass into one of the jacket pockets, took the cotton knapsack out and slung it over my shoulder. Then I crept downstairs to the kitchen, listening for sounds every step of the way. Not a noise from upstairs. I stuffed the knapsack with as many apples as it could hold. With a long knife I punched a hole through a loaf of bread, then threaded it with the carefully saved string and tied it around my neck the way children did when they brought bread to school for lunch. Next I opened the utensil drawer, took out the knife I'd chosen and tucked it into my jacket pocket.

The last thing I did before slipping out the front door was to place the haircutting scissors on the kitchen table where Madame would be sure to see them. Whether she'd understand the gesture or not, it was a message I had to give her: "I've cut myself off from you—forever."

Childishly believing that I might find my parents in Germany I headed off on foot toward what was, for me, the most dangerous place in the world.

Before and after my flight from the DeWaels' house I had no real understanding of what was going on around me in wartime Belgium and the rest of Europe. This is what I would learn much later:

In its pursuit of a world empire, Germany had already subdued hapless Austria, then rapidly went on to invade in turn Czechoslovakia, Poland, Norway and Denmark.

Early on the morning of May 10, 1940, Hitler's armies had marched into Belgium, Luxembourg and Holland, subjugating countries that had hoped to be protected by their neutrality. Belgium, where I was living with my parents at the time, surrendered in just 18 days. A month later France fell. Within a year or so after the occupation, my mother and father were taken away—whether by the Nazis or by local collaborators, I never knew, perhaps because they were illegal aliens or because my father was in the underground.

Hitler intended to create a "master race," a "pure race." To achieve his goal he planned, among other things, the slaughter of "inferiors" such as Poles and other Slavic peoples. But above all he intended to bring about the extermination of all Jews.

Being Jewish I was always at great risk. At any moment I could have joined the one and a half million children who fell victim to Hitler's scourge.

Belgium
Autumn, 1941

BE QUICK AND BE QUIET. Get over to the other side of the street and stay in the shadows. The canal isn't so far away, and the woods are just beyond. Once you reach trees, you'll be hard to find. The neighbors' houses—all dark and still, their windows black—could eyes be watching from a darkened room? Don't run yet; walk softly, on your toes. Just five or six more blocks to go...

Long open lots now separated the houses on the street.

Was anyone following me? I didn't dare look back. I began to run, block after block, my arms pumping, my feet flying, until a stabbing spasm in my side forced me to slow to a trot. Then there were no more houses, only broad open fields and—the canal.

Up ahead I could see the depot with its ruined hulks of bombed out oil tanks, lying on their sides like dinosaur ribs in the moonlight. Then the trusses of the old iron bridge, silhouetted against the milky sky—the bridge over the canal. I began running, as fast as my legs could carry me, racing toward the waterway. The road to the bridge was deeply scarred and rutted. Tires? Bombs? Stay to the shoulder to be less visible. I was running in a crouch now. Overhanging brambles scratched my face and arms but I barely felt them. When I reached the bridge, I threw myself down by the side of the road. The cool, damp grass soothed my burning face. Rolling on my back I hugged my knees to my chest and lay there gasping, my heart about to burst.

When my breathing slowed I sat up to look around. Moonlight clung to the deserted landscape like silver dust. In the distance I could see the village, my village no more, its dark chimneys low against the star-strewn sky. I held my breath and listened. No, there were no voices, no shadowy figures trailing me in the darkness. Only the muffled barking of a dog across the field and the murmuring water sounds of the channel. Up now! Over the canal and into the woods!

As I started across the bridge, I saw a few feet ahead a wide, ragged opening where a whole section had been torn away. Of course—the oil tank bombing. I had forgotten. The murky canal below glistened through a gaping hole. Even with the full moon, it was too dangerous to climb across the sections of trestle that remained. I would have to stay where I was, hiding on the bank beneath the bridge, then cross over next morning in daylight.

I suddenly realized that I was spent. The lateness of the hour, the strain of the secrecy, the fear, the frantic escape, it had all caught up with me. I ducked under the bridge, found a nearly level spot and lay down, huddled in my jacket, my knees drawn up close to my chest. The earth was cold and hard and smelled of mildew and rotting vegetation. I placed my knapsack, lumpy with apples, under my head and closed my eyes. But sleep eluded me. My heart was still pounding in my chest and my breath came in gasps. My whole body was stiff with tension.

Lying still in the dark I became aware of a hundred night noises. Every little snap made me jump, every rustle of a leaf had me wondering who or what was hiding there. I sat up again, watching, waiting. The sounds were all around me.

Something was under there with me! I stopped breathing to listen.

Suddenly I saw a dark form slide across a patch of moonlight, followed by another. Rats! scurrying under and across the broken bridge planks. I let out my breath in a burst of relief. Don't be an idiot—they're just little animals—not the DeWaels or the police coming to get you. Go to sleep.

I closed my eyes again, but the ground felt hard and bumpy through my padded winter jacket. I readjusted several more times. Then, when I finally managed to find a somewhat comfortable position, my mind wouldn't stop racing. Would Madame DeWael send the police after me? What if they caught me—would they hand me over to the Germans? She certainly didn't want me. Grandfather wanted me, but he couldn't hide me. Nobody wanted me, except my parents. And how was I ever going to find them? What would happen to me? If I did avoid being caught, how long would my food last? It was November now and the weather was damp and chilly. How could I manage without shelter in snow and bitter cold?

I closed my eyes once more and concentrated on the sounds around me...more scratching and scurrying of little animals. Soothing sounds. I liked listening to them going about their night business. Fellow creatures, keeping me company...

I didn't open my eyes till dawn. When the first light

made its way under the bridge I sat up and poked out my head. The sun was low behind the trees but the eastern sky glowed a pearly pink. I crawled on my hands and knees through low brush to the edge of the road to have a look. The scene was deserted. No one had followed me! They didn't come to drag me back. I was free, as free as that hawk wheeling great sweeping circles above my head. I had done it! The terror of the previous night dissipated like a bad dream.

In the warmth of the sun a slow mist was rising from the fields. The village chimneys breathed wisps of smoke into the soft air. Day one of my journey was at hand.

I grabbed the metal railing alongside the bridge and held on tightly with both hands as I tested the first plank with my foot. I could go some distance in safety before I came to a large section where the planks were completely gone. Underneath, the supporting braces were bent and crumpled—but they were there.

Then I made the mistake of looking down at the deep, black water below and my stomach flopped. I clung there a moment getting up the nerve to go on, then took a deep breath and began to inch my way across the dark water, hand over hand, along the twisted rails. When at last I reached solid ground on the other side I whooped for joy.

I climbed the bank and stood by the bridge for a moment looking across the channel to the village, like an escaped bird looking back at its cage. Then I turned my back on the bridge and all that lay on the other side and began walking. I could not know that I still would be walking four years hence.

As I marched along I polished off one of the apples from my knapsack and then tore a chunk of bread from the loaf around my neck. How long would my food last? I'd better ration it carefully. And I'd have to watch for water soon.

Despite my elation I knew I had to be careful. Better not go too far into the woods. Better to stay close to the road but in the protection of the trees, in case anyone looking for me came by in a wagon. No one would recognize me as a girl in this outfit, but it was best to play it safe. Am I really going east, toward Germany? I stopped and pulled the little compass from my pocket. Well, it looked like the road was heading east*ward*—more or less.

How many days did it take me to get to the first village, Overijse? It might have been a week, but after the first few days I lost track of time. In any case, it didn't matter. For me time was only day and night, sunlight and darkness. There were good weather days, when I could cover long distances easily, and chilly, rainy ones with slush and mud and clothes that wouldn't dry.

My worries and problems were all physical now. With the escape behind me, that nightmare was over. I was free. I could eat when I wanted, sleep when I wanted, go where I pleased, with no Madame DeWael to stand over me and order me around. But the earth was tilting toward winter. Without the most basic necessities—food, drink, shelter— how would I be able to survive?

The apples gave out after the first few days. The bread—which I'd carefully rationed—lasted about a week.

After it dried out, I would moisten a piece with saliva and chew it as slowly as possible, savoring each crumb. By the side of the road I found fox grapes that had turned to raisins, and I picked seeds and dried berries from bushes along the way. Knowing about poisonous wild fruits, I'd take a tiny bite and wait a while. Then if nothing happened I took a little more. I drank from any stream I happened to run across.

One day, with a dry throat and no stream in sight, I came upon a brown puddle left by the last rain. The water was murky but at least it was wet. Dipping into the surface, trying to avoid any sediment, I sipped from my palms. Not great but better than thirst.

Foraging in the woods, however, was turning out to be a poor way to feed myself. I was always a bit hungry in the DeWaels' house, but now I was famished. To make matters worse, after a week on my own, nausea, vomiting, cramps and diarrhea struck. Just keeping myself clean required an enormous effort. At times I thought my misery would over-whelm me. Then, little by little, the sickness went away, but I knew that somehow, somewhere, I'd have to find real food in order to keep going.

Each day I rose with the larks and began walking. Often I had weather fit for a pleasant stroll, not that that was what I was doing. I walked all day, staying off to the side of the road and close to thickets of trees as much as possible to avoid being noticed by farmers in their fields. When other travelers appeared I stepped into the woods. My route led me past undulating swaths of bare land where the stubs of harvested crops had been tilled back into the brown soil and brilliant green fields of winter rye, through thickets of graceful birch trees and along sparkling streams with pure icy water that tasted sweet after a long, dusty trek. Because the days were becoming shorter, in the late afternoon I would begin looking for a place to sleep.

As for camping out in the open, after a few nights of trying to get warm and comfortable in piles of leaves and branches, I discovered that pine trees made the best "beds." Their needles were softer to lie on, and quieter, than leaves from deciduous trees. They also provided the best shelter from the elements. On nights when drizzle fell on and off for hours, boughs of a large pine overhead would keep me completely dry. Still, I knew a heavy Belgian rain would drench me and the ground I slept on. And, pine tree or no, I soon would have to find a way to stay warm through the colder nights ahead.

The worst torment of all was my shoes, the little-girl pumps La DeWael had me wear. What a shame I had nothing more suitable for walking. With each kilometer, those shoes chafed more and cut deeper into my feet. As I went along, I kept telling myself, "It only hurts if you think about it. Think about Maman, about Grandfather, anything at all. Just keep walking." At the end of the day I'd take off the torturous pumps by a stream to soak the red bruises on my soles and rinse the open blisters where the leather scraped my flesh.

Days passed, nights came and went, and somehow I kept on walking, always east by my compass. Then at last: signs for Overijse. I knew it was a big village from Grandfather's maps. There would be food and drink there and maybe even shoes that didn't blister my feet. How to get them was another matter.

In the distance I spotted a farm house with a barn and several outbuildings. I approached the yard cautiously, staying off the road and well within the woods. The white-washed stone dwelling with a tile roof sat close to the road. I squatted on my heels, hidden by trees and shrubbery, and watched. Just beyond the house, I could see workers out in the field, harvesting what appeared to be cabbages. Perhaps they'd let me have some. But how to manage it? Do I just walk up to them and ask for food? There probably was no harm in trying that, but something held me back—probably Grandfather's warning not to trust people: "They can hurt you, *petite*."

Then another voice began urging: Find another way. Maybe they have fruit trees there, with windfall apples all over the ground. Go around back and see. Or you could hold out your hand like a beggar. That's it—pretend to be a mute beggar.

I took a deep breath, pulled Marthe's knitted cap down over my hair and marched resolutely across the road.

When I reached the back of the farmhouse I was startled to find a woman in an apron hanging laundry on a line. She stared at me as though she saw a ghost. I just stood there, looking back at her, hesitating to hold out my hand for food. Before I could do anything, she said:

"What do you want? What are you doing here, little girl?"

Little girl! My boy's get-up hadn't fooled her a bit. I spun around and ran back across the road and deep into the shelter of the trees.

Well, what now? There would be other houses up ahead. I would have to keep on moving, staying at the edge of the woods so as not to lose sight of the village. But the sun was setting behind me now and it would soon be getting dark. Best to go to sleep and try again in the morning.

Not a crumb left in the knapsack. I lay down, doing my best to ignore the hunger pains. How to get something to eat? I couldn't just wander into the village without some kind of plan. But no plan came to mind. I let the saliva well up in my mouth and swallowed, pretending it was milk from Grandfather's cow.

The next farmhouse sprawled at the end of a short lane. Was anyone inside? I could see several men and women working in the field behind the house. If I sneaked up to the front door now no one would spot me—that is, unless somebody was home. I waited as a horse-drawn wagon rattled down the road and around a bend, then quickly crossed the yard and went up to the front door.

No voices and no sound of movement. Through the screen door I could see a coat rack on the wall. Four or five knobs ran under a long rectangular mirror—no coats on the rack. Everyone must be outside. Had they locked the door? I lifted the latch slowly and pushed. The door swung in. I had to be fast; someone might come back at any moment.

I slipped inside, leaving the door ajar. Scarcely breathing, I hurried from the hallway into a small parlor, then peered around the corner and saw a kitchen. Still no one. I tiptoed into the kitchen and looked around. No fruit on the table, no tins of biscuits, no canning jars with vegetables in sight. No icebox there either, but on a cabinet in the corner there was a metal food larder with a grate across the front. Grandfather and Marthe had one just like it to keep perishable food away from sunlight and flies. I rushed over to it, raised the grill and grabbed the meat and cheese inside. And in the cabinet? A loaf of bread! Stuffing it all in my knapsack, I ran back through the hall, out the door and into the woods.

Later, while I sat slowly nibbling a piece of cheese and trying to make it last, I thought: the egg. There was an egg there in the larder. I could have taken it, punched a little hole in each end and sipped out the insides like Grandfather used to do. And I didn't remember to look for shoes! I certainly should have tried to find a raincoat too or something waterproof to sleep on when the ground was wet. In truth, I'd been far too frightened at the time to look for anything but food. But at least I didn't get caught. And now I did have something to eat.

I pulled the hunk of meat out of my knapsack and contemplated it. Beef—bright red and raw. I remembered how Grandfather would sample raw meat before Marthe cooked it and sometimes slip me bits to taste too. Being famished, I didn't hesitate to eat it, cooked or not. I cut a thin slice and popped it in my mouth. Delicious.

Just then I heard a rustling nearby. I jumped—people from the farmhouse on my trail? No, just a bony farm dog I'd seen wandering along the road earlier that day, relieving himself in the bushes.

"Here, my friend, do you want something to eat?" I cut off a small chunk of meat and held it out. The dog came over, took one sniff and instantly swallowed it like a pill. I ate another piece myself and by turns we finished the beef in no time. Then I stroked his ears and started to play and roughhouse the way I used to do with Rita and Ita. The poor creature, ribs sticking out like fence splats, responded by rolling on his back and wiggling with delight, then he sprang up and licked my face again and again. We set out together down the road.

When shadows lengthened and dusk crept into the tranquil woods, my scruffy companion bedded down with me and stayed the whole night long, letting me snuggle close against his warm body. This was the most comfortable night's sleep I'd had since my escape from the DeWaels'.

The dog didn't leave me until I passed beyond the village, a long distance from his farm. But later, other dogs would follow at my heels as I walked on, sharing any stolen food I happened to have on me. These animals were my only companions, friends I could talk to, with whom I could share affection. But the distance between villages and well-stocked larders could be long, and at times I had little, other than affection, to share with my animal friends.

By the time I'd passed through several villages I was better organized and more adept at getting what I needed. For instance, in one empty farmhouse I remembered to look for a raincoat. I could find only a man's slicker that was much too big for my small frame, and was about to leave empty-handed when I spotted the tablecloth on the kitchen table. It was made of oilcloth just like one at Grandfather's—a great find. Back in my hiding place in the woods I carefully cut a round hole in the center with my knife, in order to put it over my head to wear as a rain cape.

Unfortunately, when I tried out my improvised garment it was so long and floppy I kept stumbling over it. Then, with the first heavy rain, icy trickles seeped through the hole I'd made, drenching my neck and shirt. And on wet nights, the hole in the middle let up moisture from the soggy ground. Eventually I found another oilcloth to sleep on, but I still kept the first one. Rather than carry it around during the day, I rolled it up, sausage style, and wore it around my neck—an extra protection against cold and dampness.

From the next series of houses I raided I stole shoes, then, during the following weeks, a whole assortment from various farms and villages along the way. Looking back I remember that time as a sort of footwear parade. First I tried a pair of *brabançons*, the local style of wooden clogs I'd seen Grandfather wear—fine for working on the farm but ridiculously clumsy for any serious walking. I lost one whole day of travel because of them. Then I found some boys' shoes in my size. Later I came across some rubber galoshes, soft and rain-proof. To make them fit, I stuffed newspaper inside. The next morning I discovered that my feet had turned black from the newsprint. I reminded myself to add socks to my "shopping" list.

As for my little pumps, I used them as extras when the

ground was wet. One morning I found them where I had taken them off, bent and frozen, hard as rocks, and had to give them up for good. That experience taught me a valuable lesson. From that time on I always slept with my shoes on. (Today I own over three hundred pairs of shoes, and I don't need a psychiatrist to tell me why I buy so many more than I could possibly need.)

Beauty and neatness were hardly my top priorities at that time. As I crept through one house, on my way to the pantry I passed an open door and was startled to behold within the face of a wild creature watching me. I thought I had been caught in the act! It took me a second to realize that the grimy face, the wild hair and the animal eyes were none other than my own, staring back at me from a mirror.

How is it that during all those months of stealing I never got caught? It's true that I'd become shrewder, stronger and more agile than before. I was observant and had a good sense of timing. But any physical and mental strengths had to be matched by fantastic luck. As incredible as it seems now, during all that period chance was on my side, and my repeated triumphs gave me an increasing sense of pride and confidence.

As time passed I invented my own peculiar system for staking out a house, entering, taking what I needed and escaping. First, watching people move away from a house, I would silently beat out a staccato "One, two, three, four..." until I determined how many counts it took for the person to go from the house to the field or barn. Then, as I approached the house and moved around inside it, I counted up to that number again, allotting myself the same amount of time in case they came back. I even counted as I slipped items into my knapsack: "One" (the bread); "two" (the sausage); "three" (an egg), and so on.

Before going to sleep, I'd make up my list: First, some apples to clean my teeth, "nature's toothbrush," according to Grandfather. My fingernails did the job pretty well but sometimes a sliver of nail would tear off and get stuck between my teeth and drive me crazy. And I'd find some cloves to bite on for when I had a toothache. Cold weather required that I find a heavy sweater to put on under my jacket and another layer of trousers. And I'd sometimes wonder, "Maybe they'll have some strawberry jam…"

If, despite all my planning, things didn't work out perfectly, if I made mistakes—like the hole in the oilcloth or the newsprint that blackened my feet—it was always a lesson for the future.

Today people sometimes ask me whether I ever felt guilty about all the stealing I did back then. That question makes no sense to me. It's as though they are asking: "Did you regret keeping yourself alive?"

Some time later, I discovered another way of getting food, not to replace the thefts but to supplement them. I had been following a river for several days when I found myself in a small village. The streets were almost deserted, so I decided to explore a bit and came upon a collection of the most disreputable and unfortunate-looking people I had ever seen, sitting on the steps of a church. Some of the men wore double pairs of tattered trousers. Some had rags wrapped around their feet. I guessed that they must be beggars.

Not to be too proud, I looked like a beggar myself. In

the last village I'd entered a respectable housewife had shouted, "Vermin!" when she saw me lurking too near her doorway. I could fit in with that pitiful crew and beg a bit of food to appease my growling belly.

I sat quietly on the church steps a long while. Nobody came by, nothing was happening, but still the beggars waited there. Then the bells in the tower chimed and worshippers began filing out of the church. Immediately, several of the beggars started imploring them in whining tones, a mother held up her baby, and on all sides pale thin arms rose up, palms heavenward. It was as though a bunch of inert, shabby dolls had suddenly been wound up and set in motion. As it turned out, some entreaties were more successful than others.

I've always hated the idea of pleading with people, of asking anyone for anything, but after watching the beggars a few seconds, I finally held out my hand too. In a few minutes a nicely dressed man came by, smiled, bent over and gave me a coin. Money! What could I do with that? Certainly not go into a shop to buy something and have someone ask, "What are you doing here, little girl?" No, I'd give away the coin later.

Meanwhile, though I wasn't about to speak to anyone, I had to make myself understood. So when an elderly woman came within my range, I held out one palm to her and pointed to my mouth with the other hand. She paused a second, then gestured for me to wait there—as if she too were mute! She went into a nearby bake shop, came back and presented me with a flaky puff pastry with sugar on it, a couque au beurre, and a little round bread called pistolet.

Those were my only handouts that morning and, as far as I knew, would be my only food for the day, so I took only one or two precious bites and stored them in my knapsack.

I waited until the square had emptied and the beggars began to leave. One of the most pitiful among them—and one of the most successful in inspiring charity—was a legless man who got around in a little rough-hewn cart on wheels. Fascinated, I watched him slowly maneuver himself out of the square and followed as he inched his way down the street. Where was he going? Where would someone like that live?

The crippled man turned into a side street and, a few doors down, stopped at a narrow brick building. I watched him from the corner as he unlatched his door and laboriously pulled himself up and out of his cart. Then my mouth fell open when I saw him stand up in the doorway on two healthy limbs. As he turned to close the door he suddenly looked right at me. His suffering expression dissolved into a wide, knowing smile, then he disappeared inside.

What a lesson! How many of the other beggars were using such tricks? I had no idea. But, clearly, this man had fared better than I, merely sitting there like a log and holding out my hand. The next time I begged at a church I was better prepared—and more deserving of pity—with a stolen sheet ripped into rags that bound my "wounded" arm to my chest.

Winter came gently that first year and all the world's colors melted into tints and tones of gray sky and amber meadows. Great noisy constituencies of crows held raucous conventions in the cleanly-harvested fields, criticizing and blaming each other for transgressions too numerous to count. The efficiency with which they were able to forage a meal after the crops were gone gave me the idea that there might be an overlooked carrot or potato hiding in a furrow, and occasionally there was.

Sometimes I awoke from my temporary quarters under a pile of pine needles and wandered out of the woods to see that a nighttime snowfall had blanketed the hills and valleys in such brilliance that I had to squint my eyes almost closed to avoid being blinded. Haystacks in the meadows, capped with white, reminded me of sugar-dusted cream puffs in the window of the *patisserie* in Brussels. The ponds I passed, ringed with golden reeds, were only lightly glazed with ice. Wild geese had set up winter housekeeping along the banks but the snowy tracks of foxes warned that they must not sleep too soundly.

No matter how bad the weather or irritating my shoes, there was hardly a day I didn't make some headway. By conscious effort I was training myself to walk faster and to cover more miles. Sometimes, according to the road markers, I traveled over eight miles a day. And all along the way my mind propelled me on with the words, "I am going to find my parents."

My first goal was to get to the Ardennes forest. According to Grandfather's maps one could cross from Belgium into Germany by going through the Ardennes. Was I actually going in that direction? I knew nothing about navigating by the north star, but Grandfather had explained about the sun rising in the east and setting in the west, and, of course, I had my compass.

It was impossible to go in a straight line, as the crow flies—too many detours and obstacles: There were roads that wound like a bedspring and steep, rocky terrain that slowed me down and rivers that I would follow for miles in the wrong direction while looking for a bridge. I simply had to push on and hope for the best.

At some point the woods gave out and I now slept in hay stacks or fields of high grasses or in thickets of trees. Occasionally, reaching a town with too many people bustling around, I chose to hole up and sleep in a hiding place during the daytime, and then do my walking after dark. Not that I was afraid of people. It didn't bother me to walk past them or even be part of a crowd. As long as we had no conversation or confrontation I could remain an anonymous little girl off on an errand or a poor beggar child. And so I must have seemed to others. But whenever possible I simply preferred to avoid humans altogether.

People today sometimes ask, "How did you survive, a child alone like that?" I could sum it up by saying, "By disappearing." It was *because* I was a child and alone that I escaped suspicious attention. In fact, one day a German soldier handed me a piece of candy. And why wouldn't he? With my light eyes and blond hair, messy or not, I might have reminded him of his little Aryan daughter back home. I threw the candy in the gutter as soon as he was out of sight.

"La Meuse!" The sign said this river was the Meuse. I remembered Grandfather tracing it on the map all the way into the Ardennes. This had to be the right way. But when I checked my compass I was confused. It showed that by going along the river I was heading north, not east. The river had to get there eventually though, didn't it? Grandfather's map had showed it winding deep into the forest. I finally decided to keep following it, at least for a while.

I traveled along the wide river, bustling with activity, for many days. A steady stream of commerce made its way up and down—military vessels, barges, ferries, skiffs and scows. I wondered what purpose or mission each was engaged in.

To pass the time I would try to estimate how many counts it would take for the first wave from a boat's wake to reach the shore where I stood. Small boats made little wakes that barely disturbed the brown reeds along the bank. Big boats made seismic waves that slapped and splashed when they hit.

Along the river I discovered sunsets. Traveling in woods as I had been doing, the end of the day for me had been just a lessening of visibility, with perhaps some pink above the tangle of treetops overhead; then darkness. Now I could look across the sweeping expanse of shining water, all the way to the horizon. In late afternoon I would sit on the bank and watch the frozen winter sun slip down and slowly warm, then redden, until, when it dropped, it was a ball of fire, setting both the sky and the river ablaze. The barges and ferries, black cinders in the conflagration, continued to make their way along the molten current as if nothing extraordinary were happening.

Late at night when there was no wind and the river was mirror smooth, I'd see long lights from the boats stretching toward me across the water and wonder who was inside those floating rooms and what they were doing. Sometimes I'd hear drunken laughter or voices raised in anger skipping across the glassy expanse, so loud and clear I felt they were right beside me. And sometimes I'd hear nothing, as when a boat would pass silently, with no lights—for some reason, like me, it chose to go unseen. But I'd know that it had gone by, and that it was big, by the loud smacking, sucking sounds of its wake hitting the rock where I sat listening.

I had no idea where the river was going. And the walking was painful now. The clogs I was wearing cut into my feet and squeezed my toes till they were numb. It was time to get some better shoes.

I had gone only as far as the front parlor of the next empty house when I caught sight through the window of a man riding toward the house on a bicycle. That's what I needed—a bicycle—but not from here. I quickly tiptoed to the back of the house and slid out an open window and down to the ground, with no food and no shoes. Later that afternoon I had better luck. Walking along within sight of the water I noticed the loveliest smell of wood smoke and fish. Following my nose I discovered a smokehouse, and it was unlocked! Hanging from the rafters over smoldering embers were racks and racks of small, brown fishes, more than I had seen in my whole life. In a minute I had loaded my knapsack and pockets with all they could hold and was on my way again. With that fragrant cargo, I had many offers of canine (and even feline) companionship along my walk.

The problem of my shoes resolved only a short while later when I ran across just what I wanted. Across the road that ran parallel to the river I spied a bicycle, propped against a fence. It was twilight and there was no one around. I quickly snatched the bike and dragged it across the road and out of sight, where I mounted it and sped off, pushing the pedals as fast as I could. It was obviously an older child's bicycle and somewhat big for me, but for a few days it helped me make good headway.

Even before I saw the sign with a name I recognized from Grandfather's map, "Marche-en-Famenne," I knew I had reached the Ardennes. The trees now were tall and dense around me. What before had been woods became thick, dark forest. The topography had changed too. The mostly flat land I'd traveled over throughout my journey had turned to great rolling hills on all sides. The trees and the slopes were too much for the bicycle. I propped it against a tree for the next weary traveler and continued on foot. The walking was easier anyway because I had managed to snitch a pair of sturdy boots. They were too big, but I stuffed them with rags.

Going east took me away from the river and deeper into the majestic forest where I could look up and see the unbranched trees rising straight like columns in a temple till their tops touched the sky. Spears of sunlight dropped from the leafy canopy high above, dissipating in the gloom before reaching the ground. Later, I encountered deep ravines and high cliffs where streams embedded in the rock had seeped through sheer stone walls making fanciful and grotesque frozen waterfalls that cascaded without movement a hundred feet and more.

Night came early now. Snow fell, deep and soft—not a threat at all but a thrilling spectacle of nature. It clung like cotton batting to boughs and branches and spread smoothly across the rolling hills like an eiderdown comforter. From the peaks the wind lifted mists of snow powder high into the air.

Once as I was kneeling to drink from an icy stream I heard the sound of hoofbeats. It was a stampede coming toward me like a locomotive—boom!—so fast I had only a second to get out of the way. I caught but a glimpse of backsides disappearing into the brush. Boars! I stared in fascination at the tracks in the snow that was all they left behind.

For me this place was fairyland, so lovely that for a while I forgot everything and just marveled at its beauty, looking, listening to the sounds and the silence, drinking it all in. I would stand at the top of a hill and shout across the breathtaking landscape: "This is all mine, this is my home!"

Or when I relieved myself and wiped with a broad leaf, I'd sing at the top of my lungs "Lovely month of May"—a silly song Grandfather taught me:

Lovely month of May,
When will you return

With your great big leaves
So I can wipe my... Lovely month of May,
When will you return...?

Beau moi de mai
Quand reviendras-tu
Avec tes larges feuilles
Pour frotter mon ... Beau moi de mai,
Quand reviendras-tu?

And I'd smile remembering how I used to yell "ass!" every time he came to "So I can wipe my," while he just continued singing "Lovely month of May."

I eventually came upon huge swamps, called *les fagnes* (I would learn the name later), with curious milky water and sweeping stands of reeds as tall as trees. I'd walk for days and days on ground so wet it squished loudly beneath my feet. I had plenty of company here; in fact, each lake was a hectic airport. Flocks of geese would depart like huge squadrons of planes, taxiing down the watery runway with a great fanfare of honking and beating of wings, until the air caught under their flight feathers and they were airborne *en masse*. They came in the same way, all together, arching their necks, their webbed feet forward, braking against the surface of the water, until they slowed, settled gently and folded their broad wings across their backs.

These marshes were the habitat of many species of wading birds—spoonbills, ibis, egrets, herons—by the thousands, in an unending assortment of colors and sizes. The herons, flamboyant courtiers of this reedy kingdom, engaged in an avian minuet that involved a great deal of formal bowing and curtsying and flaunting of their enormous cape-like wings.

Though these waters were very broad, I knew they were shallow because the long-legged birds waded all the way across. I, however, had to be careful for the sulfurous black muck was so deep it swallowed my boots and nearly sucked them off with every step. There were animal tracks everywhere. Occasionally I would see men's tracks too; trappers, I guessed, because occasionally I would come across one of their snares. If a trapped animal were alive I would set it free, if not, I skinned it with my knife and ate it.

Once I came upon two men in the act of setting a trap. They did not see me although I almost walked right into them. They were speaking French, so I hid in the brush and listened. "Last summer in this spot I was almost eaten alive by mosquitos," one said. "The swarms were so thick around my head I could hardly see my hand before my face." The other man laughed. "This is the land of the vampires," he replied.

Fortunately for me, spring that would be bringing those bands of hungry bloodsuckers was a long time away, though I did encounter them soon enough in my travels. Then I witnessed for myself how they hovered in huge clouds and attacked without mercy until any bit of exposed skin was swollen and raw. I had no gloves for protection as I walked, pushing aside brush and reeds with my hands. At night I would suck on my bleeding flesh trying to soothe the terrible itching.

I would also encounter another swamp creature with a thirst for blood: leeches. As repulsive as they were, however, they were not terrifying to me. Bigger than my big toe, black and elastic, they lurked hungrily in the reeds awaiting an opportunity to make a meal on any living thing that passed their way, whether animal or human. I even saw them attached to the bodies of fish. When I was in an area inhabited by leeches, no matter how warm I was from exertion, I always kept myself well covered. At the end of the day I would inspect my body and often find one or two of them clinging to my garment, looking for an opening to a meal.

When the weather eventually turned mild, I was able to cover a lot of ground. After my near encounter with the trappers, I had realized that I had to be more cautious; the forest was not mine alone. From that time on I was careful not to talk or sing out loud. I grew accustomed to the quiet of the woods and became as stealthy as the animals themselves.

Over time all my senses were heightened—my vision, my hearing, even my sense of smell. That hyper-sensitivity stayed with me for a very long time after I left the forest. For example, it took many years of being back in society before I stopped whirling around when I heard footsteps behind me on the street. Even today I am easily disturbed by the noise of traffic or a radio or people talking loudly.

The forest became my home and also my school. I found its lessons everywhere. Whenever I came to a wide stream I looked for a beaver dam to get me across. But before I went on I'd always stop and sit on the bank for a while studying the beavers' activities. I was impressed by their ingenuity and industry. At dusk they emerged from their lodge to begin felling trees and remodeling their quarters and continued their labors into the wee hours. When I slept nearby, all through the night I'd hear them hissing and growling and slapping the water with their broad tails.

Sometimes I'd find cavities in the bank where their neighbors, the otters, lived. I'd keep a look-out for their little webbed tracks in the mud and occasionally come across a family of them playing in the water, tossing sticks or rocks in the air and diving after them, just like children. The otters held animated conversations of screams, whistles, scolding noises and something that sounded just like human laughter. Eventually I learned the voices and calls of all of the animals I encountered and could speak to each in its own language. I never tired of studying the wild creatures. When I came across a nest of hamsters or rabbits I'd lie on my stomach for hours, as patient and still as a cat, observing their family life.

I also developed my own domestic routines. Each night before going to sleep I "made" my bed. First, I located a large pine, one with low branches coming down like a tent. I unrolled the first oilcloth, the one with the hole in the middle, and draped it over a few lower branches. Then, with sticks and my hands, I dug out a shallow trench, piling boughs high at the sides to shelter me from the wind. On the bottom I placed more boughs and soft needles and the second oilcloth and, finally, I arranged my knapsack as a pillow and lay down.

Usually I was so tired I fell asleep immediately. But one night, for a change, I stayed wide awake, breathing in the lovely scent of my pine bed and listening to the agitated shrieks and chatters of the night creatures. Lying there I thought of so many things: How far had I traveled that day? I guessed I was making good progress. The boots I now wore weren't bad, and I always had a reserve pair tied around my neck.

Thinking about shoes reminded me of the time Madame DeWael called Grandfather a "barefoot bum," *va-nu-pieds*. On only one occasion did she go with me to the farm. As she talked to him earnestly across the kitchen table, I loitered nearby, listening as hard as I could, but catching only a few words here and there. Then at one point Grandfather slapped the table hard with his hand and said, "No butter, no potatoes, no eggs, nothing!" From what she answered, I inferred she had decided to stop my visits and he had told her, if that were the case, then he wasn't going to give her any more produce.

On the way home, Madame, furious, complained bitterly about Grandfather. I found it amusing when she kept calling him "that barefoot bum." Well, she certainly couldn't call me *va-nu-pieds* now that I'd managed to get two pairs of wearable shoes. But of course she'd never give me credit for a thing. "You'll never amount to a pile of peas," was one of her favorite accusations when she was angry with me. That was so unlike Grandfather, who'd say just the opposite: "You can do anything." Well, I was doing all right so far.

But why think about La DeWael? Think about something happy, like your parents. I wondered where they came from originally. Here I was now, making this trip, but long ago I made another long journey, in Maman's belly. She told me she and Papa had traveled in a distant country when she was pregnant with me, before arriving in Belgium. I knew my parents came from far away. But from where? She only told me they moved from one place to another, fleeing persecution. My poor parents; they were running and hiding for so long, even before I was born. And now it was my turn.

I remembered Papa spoke so many languages—Maman too. When they didn't want me to understand what they were saying, they talked in German or Yiddish or Russian instead of French, and even though I didn't comprehend the meaning of their words, I could always tell which language they were speaking. I remember Papa used to call Maman pet names in Russian, like *doucha maya*, meaning "my dear" or "my darling." But what country did they come from? Russia? And were they really in Germany now?

Papa would often go off to secret meetings, to places he never spoke about to me. Maman got upset sometimes when he left the house at night with his friend Gilles. One night I heard her say, "It's dangerous. I don't want you to go." She looked so unhappy, I chimed in, "Papa, stay home, stay home!" Then Gilles said, "All right, little one, you don't want us to leave? Here's what we'll do: I'll stay here and keep your mother company." He put his arm around Maman and pretended to snuggle up to her. I was so angry at that, I pulled him away from her with both hands and shouted, "No! Go!"

I was closest to Maman because we were alone together so much—Maman with her black hair, dark eyes, smooth olive skin. Papa was fair, like me. That must be why it was always he who went with me to school. With our blond hair and light eyes and the false name we used, we were never taken for Jewish. Maman wouldn't have wanted to put me in danger by being seen with me in public.

Maman, Maman—my longing for her was an anguish that cut deep into my heart.

An owl hooted gently in the branches above me and I turned over in my soft, fragrant bed. I am surrounded by all this beauty, I thought, yet I am alone. I am as lonely as if I were the only human alive on the whole face of the earth. My empty stomach growled and an infected wood splinter in my hand throbbed painfully. I began caressing my earlobe as if it were Maman's and making the sucking noises I made before falling asleep in their bed.

CHAPTER 3

Germany
Winter, 1942

I HAD BEEN TRAVELING FOR A LONG TIME through a dense, primeval forest, surviving on acorns, needles and sap from spruce trees and little white grubs that I dug from deep beneath the forest's matted carpet. Now I was beginning to see signs of human life, a cabin here and there, a wagon trail. As I walked along the edge of a narrow lane, I heard laborers speaking German, not with Grandfather's French accent but the real German my father spoke. I realized I must have crossed into Germany at some point while I was traveling through deep woods.

I was now in enemy territory. I remembered the blue line on Grandfather's map representing a big river in Germany. I knew if I kept going eastward I would eventually come to it so I followed a heavily trafficked highway at a distance until it led to a wide expanse of water. And then, there it was before me: I had reached the Rhine.

But I was now stuck. I could go no farther because I was afraid to cross where there was so much traffic. I don't know how long I followed the river looking for a way to get across—many days. When at last I came to a narrower, less traveled bridge, I waited until the middle of the night and then ran across and hid in the woods on the other side. It was several days later that I came to the outskirts of a town where the houses looked prosperous enough to have something decent to eat in their pantries.

As I approached, I thought of the kitchens I had raided in Belgium. It would be good to find real food again. I began to imagine fat sausages and fresh eggs in empty larders and barrels of sauerkraut and pickles in dark cellars—all waiting for me to help myself. In a moment of weakness I turned onto the main road leading into town.

As I approached the market area, the townspeople I passed seemed ordinary enough—young mothers with pink-cheeked babies, rustic farmers in town to buy supplies, harried merchants, dapper businessmen, clerks and shop girls, all going about their errands in a humdrum way. Absorbed in their own affairs, they took no notice at all of me. But I quickly realized what a mistake I'd made when I began to observe everywhere around me—on stone walls, on doors and shutters, on houses, on the sides of wagons, even on the pavement, neatly stenciled in red paint—swastikas. In a vacant lot I came upon a band of little boys playing soldier. I understood too well the words they were shouting, "Heil, Hitler!" I'd heard them many times when Leopold and his buddies imitated the Nazis. In this unremarkable village hatred had such an ordinary face.

Standing there on the bustling street, I suddenly couldn't breathe. My heart began to pound against my ribs and a cold sweat soaked the skin under my shirt. I was passing unnoticed for the moment, but I felt like a bird in a sea of voracious cats. I veered quickly down an ally and out the other side into the nearest thicket of trees, then broke into a run and headed for the woods.

Back in the relative safety of the forest I was filled with despair. How could I ever find my parents in this terrifying country? It seemed impossible when I couldn't venture near populated areas to look for them. Still I had no choice but to go forward. If I could just keep going, perhaps something would turn up.

After that frightening experience I avoided populated areas at any cost, staying deep in the woods, venturing out only occasionally to scrabble an overlooked potato or turnip from a farmer's field. Occasionally I would come upon an isolated cabin, but I no longer felt confident ducking in and out to snitch food and clothing. Instead I waited and watched for a long time before entering. In Belgium I had pulled my capers with bravado, even when the residents were just outside the kitchen window where I stood stuffing my sack with their dinner. Now, when assessing a possible target, there were many times when I would decide the risk was too great. My stomach growled constantly, but fear held the upper hand over hunger.

I was always on the lookout for safe apple trees, the ones that had been abandoned to the wild; well-tended orchards were too risky to raid. Although it was relatively safer to steal crops from the fields than food from houses, foraging was no picnic. After the crops were in, all that was left were barren furrows teeming with mice. Gleaning a meal from rows already harvested a second time by wild creatures was slow going. I had to make my move when it was still night, at first light actually, and be in and out in minutes. Only rarely was I willing to risk being exposed for the time it took to find a meager morsel. Even then, I was so terrified of being caught I could barely concentrate on the search and so I usually came away with slim pickings.

When the nights turned bitter cold, I would look for a barn where I could hide for a few hours to keep warm. I had to be very careful not to disturb the animals; my stealthy arrival made them react to me as if I were a predator and they would begin to protest loudly. I learned that, once they became aware of me, it was better not to creep around but to move deliberately and confidently as if I were on some business completely unrelated to them. If I thought it was safe, I would lie down for a few hours near a dozing cow or sheep. I myself slept so lightly that I heard every tiny noise and I'd rise to depart long before the first cock's crow. I was immensely grateful for those short moments of warmth.

As the winter wore on, my desperation often led me to barnyards where I'd scrounge animal fodder, even swill set down for a pig. I would go up to a trough the height of a pig's snout, close my eyes tight, hold my breath, then bury my face in a stew that looked like vomit—and swallow. Sometimes I'd see a cow watching my strange performance, rolling her eyes under long, straight lashes until the whites showed in alarm. Before I made my exit I would say to my hosts, "Thanks for sharing with me; you're more generous than the humans I know."

Once or twice I was lucky to come across a quantity of pork hocks hung up to cure. I'd taken some from a farmhouse in an Ardennes village and knew how useful they could be, not just for the meat but also for the thick, fatty layer under the rind. You could rub the fat on your face to prevent chapping and smear your soles with it or put a layer of it inside your shoe, to keep your feet from getting sore. The rind itself was also useful. You could chew on it all day long, sucking out the fat with its delicious smoky flavor. Naturally, Grandfather had something to say on that subject too: "Every part of the pig is useful, outside and inside. And you can eat the meat, the skin, the trotters and all."

When I left Belgium I was sinewy and strong, I'd had food in my knapsack and flesh on my bones. But finding something to eat was becoming almost impossible. I was ravenous all the time. The gnawing in my belly never let up. In desperation I dug earthworms from under deep piles of rotting vegetation and swallowed them whole. Sometimes I chewed brown leaves. Though a poor substitute for a meal, chewing could at least give me the illusion of eating.

Once, crazed with hunger, I got down on my hands and knees and scooped dirt from the ground into my mouth. Tears of sorrow, tears of rage at my circumstances, tears of despair ran down my cheeks and into my mouth and mixed with the sweet, sandy loam. Grit stuck between my teeth for a long time, but worse, a short while later I vomited. Better to endure the hunger than try that again. Even better to go to sleep. As Grandfather used to say, "He who sleeps eats," meaning that when you are not awake you don't know you are hungry.

Can one grow accustomed to starving? I'd say so. After a while the hole in the pit of my stomach became second nature to me, a dull pain that accompanied me everywhere. But I noticed that my clothes were hanging like a scarecrow's on my body.

So many problems. Many weeks ago in the Ardennes, I'd gone through lots of snow with almost no physical discomfort. Now the weather had turned colder than anything I could ever remember in Belgium. My hands became so gnarled and raw they looked like an old woman's. My lips were scabbed and blistered from the cold; they would have split and bled if I smiled. That never became a problem for I had nothing whatever to smile about. I yearned for the Belgian butter that had protected my skin last fall. Whenever I'd found a butter crock in a kitchen I would scoop it out with my fingers, eat my fill then smear it all over my face and hands.

I don't know which posed the bigger problem, my stomach or my feet. I tried always to be careful where I walked in order to avoid getting my boots wet, but no matter how cautious I was, I would occasionally step into what appeared to be a pile of leaves or a mound of snow only to have it collapse under my weight into an icy puddle. I had extra boots tied around my neck, but if both pairs got wet I knew that I would have many days of excruciating pain ahead of me until they dried out. Dampness caused swelling and open sores that coated the inside of my boots with sticky blood.

All my layers of clothing and rags in my boots were no match for the temperature and the wind. I always slept with my boots on, but one morning when I checked to see why my toes were numb, I realized there was something wrong. They looked waxy and yellow and stayed icy cold when I rubbed them between my palms. I sat cross-legged with my feet up under my trousers against my bare calves until my toes finally warmed up. On bitter cold nights I took to wrapping my feet in a sweater, putting them into my knapsack and pulling my coat down over them.

I discovered a better way to protect my toes from frostbite when I saw a dozen or so crows gathered around something in a field. My first thought was: Did they have anything to eat that I could share? As I approached, the crows took off, leaving on the ground the object of their interest—a dead hare, nearly intact. I picked up the little corpse and hurried back into the woods, pleased with my unexpected dinner. As I began to cut the meat away from the bone I realized I had won myself a bonus that would last far longer than this meal—the hare's soft, thick pelt. Carefully I peeled the hide from the carcass, scraped it clean with the blade of my knife, cut it in half and stuffed a piece of fur into each boot.

Even now with those times behind me, whenever I see sheets of ice coating the hard winter ground, a shudder runs through me as I remember those nights. It seems incredible to me now that I actually fell asleep in such temperatures and endured those punishing ordeals without succumbing to pneumonia or frostbite. Yet it's true that others, in concentration camps, were exposed to far worse than that—forced to stand naked in temperatures of twenty below, their bare feet deep in snow—and some of them survived.

When I came to the end of the forest I lost my protective cover and was forced to do what I had avoided all along—walk down open roads and go across bare fields within sight of dwellings. It was lucky for me that spring plowing had not yet begun so the fields were not crawling with farm workers. Occasionally I would see uniformed motorcyclists or a convoy of military vehicles but I rarely encountered men walking along the roads. I guess that most of the able-bodied had gone off with the invasion forces. And of those folks still around, why would they take any notice of a solitary little girl, walking along, minding her own business?

My invisibility was no accident. Since entering Germany I had perfected the art of being transparent, a skill that would save my life at least a thousand times during the course of my journey. Yet despite my unremarkable appearance, I was preternaturally shrewd. I had developed the habit of moving silently, seeing out of the back of my head and hearing through my pores. I steered clear of people whenever I could, which was most of the time. In the woods, if I heard voices or saw human tracks, I'd climb a tree and hide until the birds and other forest creatures began to chatter again signaling that the danger had passed. Like a raccoon I watched as people passed right below me, never looking up.

When I was forced to travel within view of people they never noticed me, I learned, so long as I avoided making eye contact or letting them know I was aware of them. I always moved in a purposeful way that suggested that I belonged where I was, that nothing was amiss where I was concerned.

And, when necessary, I could run as fast as a hare into the brush and disappear, for I had strong, sinewy legs.

With my fair coloring and my otherwise harmless mien, I trusted that people spotting me from some distance wouldn't think twice. But now my clothes were torn rags, crusty with mud, my face was chapped raw and my dirty hair was full of lice and matted with burrs and twigs. I dug at my itching scalp with my nails and ate whatever I was able to scratch off—that's how hungry I was. In my present condition if someone saw me up close, I would certainly arouse suspicion. Yet there was no way I could keep myself clean. Bathe in frozen ponds? Change my clothes more often? How?

There was only one solution to the problem of my appearance: I had to do all my walking and foraging after dark. I had traveled that way before, but not often, and then only when a smooth road and a big moon made it easier. I was determined to keep moving no matter how black the night or rough the terrain. My eyes became accustomed to the dark after only a couple of rough outings, and I learned to move swiftly and surely, even without the assistance of a full moon.

Even better, when I came across railroad tracks running east, I was able to follow the gleaming rails for miles and miles, covering ground just as well as I could by daylight. In the black of night I'd feel trembling in the steel and see a pinpoint of light in the distance and then would come a distant rumble, and in less than a minute a long train would roar by, striking sparks from the rails and hurling cinders into my eyes. After it passed I felt more alone than ever.

The only bright moments I ever had were when I was lucky enough to run into stray dogs. German though they were, they accepted me with as much affection as the ones in Belgium, though now I had no food to share. Often they would walk with me for long distances, as glad to have company as I. Since I had no human companionship, no one to talk to, with whom to share the burdens of my heart, it became my habit to chat with them as I would with a friend, as if they understood everything I said. Occasionally one of these strays would lie down beside me for the night, as the Belgian dogs had done. Those moments of warmth and solace were few and far between. Most nights I was alone in the dark and the bitter cold.

It was the sound of barking, however, that lured me into danger. I had been walking for weeks without meeting a friendly dog. One morning I was trudging through the wintry woods hoping I would come across a stray mongrel soon. The weather that day had turned unseasonably mild and a thick white fog engulfed the landscape so that I could see only a few feet in front of me. Wrapped in this moist shroud I was feeling particularly isolated and disoriented. In the distance, curiously muffled by the cottony haze, I could just make out the excited yapping of dogs.

My spirits lifted with the possibility of meeting up with a friendly canine face and I quickened my steps. The barking grew louder and I could make out that the forest ended just ahead of me. I slowed my pace and, peering through the mist, made an unexpected discovery—the barking was coming from inside a tall fence constructed of many rows of barbed wire, stretching as far as I could see, and on one post a sign: VERBOTEN. A shot of terror like an electric shock went through me and I instantly spun around and fled. I had no idea what I had stumbled upon but I knew instinctively I was in a dangerous place. Later, I realized that this probably was one of the many Nazi camps in the kingdom of death where "undesirables" including Jews, intellectuals, Gypsies, political opponents and homosexuals were held as slave laborers (and guarded by dogs) until they died by starvation or disease or were shipped off to the gas chambers.

The German winter was pitiless and I often thought that I would freeze or starve to death. The creatures of the forest, I could tell, were almost as desperate as I for, during particularly harsh stretches of weather, I'd sometimes find little frozen carcasses of mice and birds lying on the ground, a windfall meal for me. From every tree and bush the lower growth had been nibbled away as high up as a deer could reach standing on its hind legs. Deer tracks in the snow were a common sight, though I rarely saw the animals who left them. Hunters had made them wary of the scent of humans. Sometimes I saw the hunters' tracks too. In fact, I saw human tracks often enough to know that I had to be cautious at every moment, even in the densest forest.

The icy teeth of winter gnawed relentlessly on my fingers and toes, bit through the skin and ground into the little bones. One night I was so cold I thought if I went to sleep I might freeze in that spot and never wake up. Needles of sleet were pelting the brittle trees over my head and the boughs I had arranged to shelter me for the night. Moisture seeped under my oilcloth and clung to my thin ribs; my feet, too, were damp and I was shivering uncontrollably. I packed up my bed and began trudging, my feet following the depressions in a rutted wagon road.

The night was black as pitch, but up ahead I could see a point of light emanating from a distant farmhouse. Perhaps there would be a barn or shed where I could find shelter from the storm. Blinking away ice crystals, I fixed my eyes on the faint orange beacon as I plodded stiffly on. Through the sleet, a searing wind brought the sweet smell of wood smoke. When I came to a path leading up to the glowing windows I turned in and approached cautiously. A small, low dwelling occupied the center of the hilltop clearing and nearby stood a tall fir tree. I crept across the clearing and squatted beneath its branches.

All around me fine pellets of ice hissed angrily as they struck the earth, frozen hard as a sheet of steel. Inside the little house, a fire roared and its red-gold light leapt through the window panes and into the bare trees outside, where it darted from branch to branch. I sucked on my numb fingers trying to warm them. The taunting fragrance of burning wood froze in my nostrils and I was nearly overcome with a feeling of intense longing.

I watched that window for a long time thinking, "A family is inside there, cozy and warm, and I am out here, starving and cold and all alone. Why?"

The next morning the world was encrusted with dia-
monds. Every bony branch, every leafless twig, every shriveled brown stem seemed to have been dipped, like a candle
wick, into the clearest glass. The sun's first rays flowed like
a current through the icy trees and the whole world
sparkled and glittered. All this beauty was lost on me; I was
almost dead from cold.

I survived that night and many more. Each and every
day I rose and walked onward, except when the weather
was too harsh and then I holed up in whatever shelter I
could find and slept curled in a tight little ball waiting for
the weather to improve. But I was growing more despon-
dent with each passing day. Traveling across Germany, seeing well-manicured farms and tidy villages with rows of
houses outlined with white picket fences, so snug, so neat
and so pretty, it was hard to imagine that this country was
in the midst of a war. I decided Germany had to be the win-
ner because, from the looks of things, these people didn't
know hardship. Their apparent success made my quest to
find my parents seem all the more foolhardy.

The all-too-familiar conundrum spun around in my head
again: What chance had I to find my parents in that enemy
country? Blond or not, I couldn't simply walk into a village
and try to talk to people. On the other hand, what point
would there be in turning back after coming all this way? Go
back through that terrifying country? And what would I be
returning to anyhow? Grandfather couldn't take me back.
There were no welcoming arms awaiting me there. And I
certainly couldn't stop; to stay in one spot was to risk being
noticed. No, better to go on, say just up to that next knoll,

and then think about what to do. And after that hill it was "just up to" some other landmark in the distance. And so I continued trekking ahead without once turning back.

One day, with not a crumb to eat in my knapsack, I was chewing on a twig as I walked through a grove bordering a field. As usual when I was famished, visions of wonders I had eaten long ago swirled in my head—the whole ham I'd once stolen, the thick buttermilk and potato soup Marthe made, dark, creamy chocolates Grandfather once gave me. As I looked around hopelessly for some dried berries or seeds to eat I heard singing. Singing in French, not German!

But one day of our life
Spring will return in full flower.
Liberty, dear Liberty
Some day you'll be mine...

Mais un jour de notre vie
Le printemps refleurira.
Liberté, Liberté chérie
Je dirai tu es a moi

I moved in the direction of the song and peered out through the trees. Two men were standing in a field, both wearing caps and long trench coats. They were laborers of some kind—the one who was singing was leaning on a spade. Were they prisoners of the Germans?

I was starving and they spoke my language, that was enough to screw up my courage. I stepped out into the open and waited.

"Hey, look at the kid," the man with the spade said, and he started to address me in German.

I shook my head "No."

"What does she want?" the other man asked him in French.

I pointed to my mouth to indicate "food."

"Oh, you understand French?"

I nodded "Yes."

They started asking me question after question, but despite our common language, I refused to break my silence. The man with the spade tried repeatedly to get information from me. He asked if I was French, if I was by myself, if I'd escaped from someplace, and at one point he even inquired if I was Jewish. All he learned from my "yes" and "no" nods was that I was alone and that I was hungry.

Still, he must have guessed something, for at one point he asked, "Where are your parents?"

I shrugged my shoulders.

"You don't know? Are you trying to find them?"

I said nothing, but could feel the tears welling up in my eyes.

"Listen, child, if you're looking for somebody, there's nobody left here. They're over there," he said, pointing with his spade, "to the east."

Saying that, he kicked some objects toward me across the ground—two large, muddy potatoes. I stared at them. Was he giving them to me?

"Now take them and get out fast."

I grabbed the potatoes and ran back to the woods. Dirt and all, the potatoes were gone in a minute, but that phrase "to the east" became my talisman for weeks to come. I would continue walking "to the east."

My habit of never speaking was a detriment in that I couldn't ask for help or information. Today, however, I realize that it was also one of the keys to my survival. Not understanding the languages of the countries I passed through, I was unable to listen in on people's conversations to determine who was friend and who was foe, so I just assumed everyone was the enemy. More important, because I spoke only French, there was nothing to be gained and everything to be lost by opening my mouth and calling attention to myself as a foreigner.

Nearly six months had passed at the time I encountered those two French-speaking laborers (who were probably prisoners of war) and I was a long way from where I'd begun my journey. Some days I was able to make good headway and others very little, but all in all I estimate that I usually walked five or six miles a day.

Always an outsider, just passing through, I was nevertheless a keen observer. In fact, my naive assumption that Germany was winning the war was correct at that time. After Hitler's surprise attack on Russia in June, 1941, the Red army retaliated with fierce counter-offensives. But despite the Russians' inroads and the growing resistance movement throughout Europe and the East, the occupied countries were powerless against the Germans.

Another surprise attack, the Japanese bombing of the US Pacific Fleet at Pearl Harbor on December 7, 1941, at last drew the reluctant Americans into the war. Britain now had a powerful ally against the Germans, although America's strained resources at that time could not yet support a major campaign in Europe.

The long struggle would continue.

CHAPTER 4

Poland
Spring, 1942

MAKING IT ACROSS THE GERMAN BORDER would do little to improve my chances of survival, for anti-Semitism was nearly as virulent in Poland as it was in the fatherland of the Third Reich. In fact, during the early stages of Hitler's campaign, many Poles approved of his condemnation of the Jews and were pleased, some openly, others secretly, to see their Jewish neighbors rounded up and hauled away. Much later I learned this, and the economic reason for the Poles' attitude: For very little money, they could buy up all that the departed Jews had possessed—their jewelry, clothing, household goods, homes and businesses. Even after the war when those few Jews who had survived returned to Poland, many faced this welcome: "You dirty Jews. You are like rats; the more one kills, the more keep coming." Those who had benefited at the Jews' expense, of course, had no wish to return what had been stolen. Ironically, Hitler regarded the Poles with almost as much contempt as he did the Jews, and so they also suffered bitterly and died at the hands of the Nazis.

Church bells pealing—a lovely sound—summoning the faithful to worship, signaling to the hollow-of-belly that pantries of good Catholics everywhere would be, for this sacred hour, unattended. The bells always gave the right signal: easy pickings.

Finally, they were leaving the house—a tiny lady in black with a shawl over her head, then a stooped man with a walking stick and, a second later, a younger fellow.

I'd been listening to the bells and watching this house, with a stork nest against its chimney, from a safe distance. They were going off now, the men in their dark hats and jackets, the woman in her Sunday best. Now's my chance; I started to rise. The woman suddenly turned and headed back into the house. What had she forgotten? The younger man shouted something to her and the wind carried his voice to me. What was he saying? Something in Polish. Within the last few days I'd overheard farm hands in the fields using a strange language that I knew wasn't German. I must have crossed into Poland.

The woman emerged from the house and the three disappeared around a bend in the road. I began moving down the path that crossed a wide brook. The water was shallow and I got across easily, stepping from one rock to another, and quickly reached the back door of the farmhouse. Only the jackdaws in the tree tops observed me slipping inside.

The kitchen was neat and clean. By the enamel sink sat a pail of buttermilk covered with a fresh linen cloth. I dipped a cup into the milk again and again, pouring it into my mouth and letting it run down my chin. Oh, it was good! I leisurely stuffed my knapsack with sausages, a chunk of yellow cheese and some black bread. I didn't bother with my counting routine because Mass always took a long time. Then there I was outside, in the spring sunshine, with enough food to fill me up.

It was such a beautiful morning. I hoisted myself up on the roof of a low shed, a perfect lookout perch just in case anyone came back early. I smiled to myself, remembering how hurried my thefts had been in Germany. Now, with the coming of spring, my confidence was back. The sun poured over my head and shoulders like warm honey. I held up my face to the breeze as if to my own mother's kisses. What a day!

A haughty rooster was doing a solitary tango across the yard, neck arched, head snapping from side to side, placing his long yellow toes precisely and with great importance. I sliced off a chunk of bread and a piece of cheese and made myself a sandwich, then lay back on the roof to eat it while I contemplated the sky. Feathery clouds drifted overhead and a buzzard rode the air currents so far up I could barely follow him. The heat from the sun-warmed roof seeped into my shoulders and back. Magpies chattered, flies droned, a woodpecker drilled a tree, the sun rose higher in the heavens and I dozed off.

Suddenly: a jolt! I was flat on my back on the ground. Two viselike hands had grabbed my ankles and jerked me off the roof. I was looking into the flushed and angry face of a farm hand who had me pinned to the ground under his knee. In a split second I pulled out my knife and lunged at him, stabbing at his neck, his chest, whatever part I could get at. He looked more amazed than alarmed, but my last stab hit home and made him fall back. I twisted out of his reach, jumped to my feet and began running as fast as I could, back toward the stream and the woods beyond.

He was following right behind me, shouting in his foreign tongue, as I reached the stream. Panicking, I tried to run across, slipped on the rocks and fell flat on my stomach with a hard thud. I felt a stabbing pain in one knee, but I pulled myself up, wet and dripping, and finally managed to get across. Looking back, I saw that the man had stopped on the other side and picked up something from the ground. I was racing with all my strength for the woods when I felt a staggering blow. The man had hurled something at me, something heavy that caught me square in the back.

For an instant I fell to my knees, but I knew I had to keep going, to get out of his sight. Driven by terror, I pulled myself off the ground and hurtled on. I scrambled up the hill on all fours. At the crest, I turned around to see where he was and spied him still at the edge of the stream. He was shaking his fist at me, but had given up the chase.

It was only then that I felt the excruciating pain in the middle of my back. Bent over in agony I managed to drag myself into the protection of the trees where I fell to the ground. Stunned and gasping, I lay there for several minutes until the thought occurred to me that I had to be sure I was not followed. I sat up slowly and looked around. Nobody. Still, my instinct told me to move away from there. I pulled myself up onto my hands and knees and painfully crawled deeper into the woods.

At last I came to a cool, dark glen, peaceful as a graveyard. I was alone. I took a deep, slow breath and held it. Then crouching there I heard myself suddenly let out a howl—not a sob, not a groan, but a howl as I had never made in my life. It was a long involuntary cry of distress, for the pain in my back, yes, but also for all my other pains—the loss of my parents, the loneliness, the hunger, the injustice. All of these together rose like a siren from the pit of my stomach to the heavens above. After a few minutes I fell quiet and just sat huddled in silence for a long time, hugging my knees, my head cradled in my arms, feeling nothing but the ache in my back.

Suddenly every muscle in my body tensed and the hair on my arms prickled. What's that? Who's there?—behind me, watching me! Slowly I lifted my head and looked over my shoulder. There, just a few feet in back of me, stood a splendid creature, studying me curiously. It was a long, thin dog—gray, shaggy and twice my size. I was struck immediately by its beautiful face: high cheekbones, an upturned nose, large, erect ears, and beautiful eyes.

What was it doing there, a wild dog roaming the woods? It was such a welcome sight that I momentarily forgot my injury and reached out to the stranger.

"Where did you come from?" I remembered the food in my knapsack. "Here, I have some meat for you." I doubled over in pain.

When I finally could raise myself a little, I cut off a piece of sausage and put it on the ground by my side hoping the dog would come nearer. But it didn't move. I cooed in my gentlest voice, "Come on, come on, it's for you. Here, it's good meat. Won't you come and get it?"

What color were those eyes? Yellow, lined all around with black, like make-up, and tilted up at the outer corners. When I looked into its eyes, however, the animal quickly turned its face away.

"You won't come? But it's so good. Here, I'll push it a little closer to you."

It seemed like hours that I was sitting there, nursing my backache and waiting for the animal to take my offering. At one point it began slowly circling me at a distance, head up, ears forward, as if to see what I was all about. I pretended not to notice and just waited. The afternoon stretched on, the shadows lengthened and finally at dusk the animal suddenly ducked forward and snatched up the meat. Then it disappeared into the shadows, and I curled up right there, trying to forget the pain and go to sleep.

The next morning I had to force myself to get up, to ignore the throbbing in my back and move on. But I couldn't get that animal out of my mind. It was wandering the woods with no home or family, a loner like me. Such striking eyes, such an intelligent expression. It must have been attracted by my crying. Perhaps if I did it again...? I stopped and let out a long "Oooooooh" but—not a sign of my dog. I walked on.

I stayed in the woods that day, not inclined to venture out near humans any time soon. Despite my discomfort I managed to walk eastward through the trees and brush for several hours, stopping frequently to rest my back. Later, toward the end of the afternoon, I came to a wide clearing ringed with gently rolling hills. As I gazed across I heard a long, lonely howl and turned to see at the crest of a distant hill—that dog! I was so delighted I howled back, trying to make exactly the same sound, starting with low yelps, sliding up to a high soprano, then letting my voice go lower and fade away. For a minute or so we exchanged greetings. Every time I tried to imitate its "Ooooooh," it responded in a new and different voice. Then it turned, trotted off in the opposite direction and disappeared.

I continued walking ahead, thinking about the animal's haunting cry. It was then that the realization dawned on me that my companion might be not a dog, but a wolf! Well, if it was a wolf it was a terribly thin one. Perhaps that was why it had ventured so near the edge of the forest where we met. Was it, like me, hoping to pilfer a meal from a barnyard?

Once or twice the next morning I saw the wolf through the trees, but the shadowy gray form quickly disappeared, and didn't show up again all that day. For the next several days it would turn up at the most unexpected moments and occasionally I would hear its eerie cry, and answer with my own. Each time it appeared it stayed in my sight a bit longer and the distance between us became less, until one morning as I was leaning over to drink from a clear pond, it appeared and we lapped water side by side—then it was gone.

Later, when evening came I found a suitable pine, dug out my den and bedded down for the night. Just as I was closing my eyes, I spied the wolf lying nearby, between two bushes. Its ears were cocked forward, its paws extended toward me on the ground, and its jewel eyes were fixed unwaveringly upon me. I raised my head slowly.

"Back again? I'm glad you're here."

The animal didn't move. I put my head down on my knapsack and lay very still. A little while later, just as I was dozing off, I saw it edge a little closer, and curl up in a tight ball several feet away. The next morning when I awoke it was gone.

I continued to see my friend in the distance from time to time as I walked along. We were both solitary travelers, hungry, lonely and in need of a friend. On the following days the wolf would appear from out of nowhere at sunset and lie down a little distance from my oilcloth bed. Eventually we were close enough to each other that I was able to tell that my companion was female. At last, after many more days and nights, she lay down right beside me. Once, before going to sleep, I tried to put my arm around her but she immediately growled and bared her teeth. Slowly, carefully, I lifted my arm.

"I'm sorry. You don't like that. That's all right."

From then on we slept back to back, her shaggy body keeping me warm on cold nights. I called her "Rita" after Grandfather's female spaniel.

In time we set up housekeeping, such as it was, at the crest of a shrubby knoll. My friend had made a shallow den under an outcropping of rock, and I dug it wider so it would accommodate two. At daybreak we awoke together. She would rise and shake the twigs from her fur, then stretch her long back and yawn ceremoniously. She was relaxed in the morning and would allow me to scratch behind her ears while her eyes got dreamy with pleasure.

Then, with me behind her, she would set off for the nearest stream to get a drink, sniffing the trail and squatting now and then to relieve herself and mark her ground. Then she would be gone without a backward glance, and I might not see her again for several hours or even a whole day. In the meantime I would go about my own task of finding an unguarded kitchen or a field with vegetables ready to pick.

One afternoon I came back early with my knapsack full of little cabbage sprouts, not ready for harvest but fine for me. I stashed them in my bed and went to the nearby stream to soak my sore feet. As I was sitting in the grass wiggling my toes in the cool water, my friend appeared on the other bank. From her jaws hung the partially eaten body of a gray hare. Of course I knew that she was off hunting when she was gone from me, but I had never before seen her with a kill. She stood there, her head high, looking very proud of herself indeed. Her early return was a happy surprise and I greeted her as I often did, by rolling on my back the way Rita and Ita had welcomed me.

She waded across the stream, carefully set down the hare right beside me, then backed up and sat on her haunches watching me intently. What a gift! My skinny friend was giving up her dinner to feed me! I picked up the hare and began chewing on the flesh. It was delicious. (To this day hare is still my favorite meat, but now cooked, of course.) As I was eating, she lay down nearby and rested her head on her front paws, her eyes on me approvingly. I gnawed on the ends of the bones and sucked out the marrow then returned what I could not chew to her to finish off. When I was done she rose and came over to me and slowly licked my face, cleaning off the last traces of blood. She did this so gently each stroke of her warm tongue felt like a kiss.

This was the first time a wolf brought me a kill, but it would not be the last.

Spring glided over the landscape as softly as a swan across a lake. In the mornings there was a sheen of dew over everything. I was a child without crayons or a paint box but I would trace pictures with my finger on huge swamp-cabbage leaves and watch the damp bloom break into drops of water and run off in tiny rivulets. Once I came across a patch of wild violets so thick that the ground seemed to be spread with a robe of royal purple. I rolled back and forth and turned somersaults on them, releasing their exquisite fragrance.

Every day as I walked I drank in the loveliness of the countryside. Stands of white birches flourished along the banks of streams. They were as supple as a corps of ballerinas, their slender trunks identically inclined, their frilly, weeping branches swaying like pale green tutus. At their feet the ground was spread with emerald moss as fine and soft as a puppy's muzzle.

Far away from the tutelage of man where I had learned so much about ugliness, the world disclosed itself to me in all its fullness and beauty. I was a child in the garden of Eden, making my way through an isolated and unspoiled wilderness.

After a long day I sat completely hidden under the trailing branches of a pond willow and watched the skittery flight of bats as they harvested their dinner of mosquitoes. Shimmering scrims of twilight descended across the landscape—

rose, mauve, deep purple, and then utter darkness over all. Soon the horizon lightened and the moon rose over the tree-tops and ascended into the star-blasted heavens, above the din of ecstatic frogs celebrating spring.

My friend had been gone for several days and I was worried about her. I had been out rustling a few speckled eggs from a nearby rookery and some big, white sugar beets from a bin in a barn. I had taken my booty into the forest to save for later. That afternoon she appeared out of nowhere—with a companion of her own, a large, black male wolf. The newcomer raised his hackles as soon as he saw me, then lowered his head, neck extended, and began to advance slowly. For a second I thought he was going to attack and I instinctively dropped to the ground and froze. My friend quickly moved between us, but the newcomer stood his ground while I held my breath. After a long moment he turned his face away, slowly backed off and walked stiff-legged to a nearby tree where he lifted his leg and peed in disdain. I could breathe again.

Seeing how my companion protected me from the big male I realized that she thought of me as a puppy, her puppy. She'd come to me upon hearing my howl of pain, she'd stayed near me these many weeks, and now she'd brought her mate to introduce us to each other. My heart filled with love and gratitude.

Until then "Maman" was a name I could give no one but my real mother, but just now this protective animal was the closest thing I had to a mother. From that time on I called her "Maman Rita." And though I continued to walk on each day with the quest for my parents in mind, I was careful not to lose her.

In spite of her new companion, whom I quickly dubbed "Ita," Maman Rita saved a place in her life for me. Returning after being gone for many hours or even a whole day, she would greet me by trotting right up to me, head down, tail wagging, and nuzzling her beautiful face against mine. When she was out of sight it was comforting to know she wasn't far away, and every time we met again I felt a surge of joy.

Ita's arrival did bring some changes though. Until he came Maman Rita and I had shared our food easily and without obvious protocol. She often encouraged me to eat first, as appropriate for a puppy. But now mealtimes were different. One afternoon I saw the male kill a fat badger that had scurried into the open. I went over to join him in the feast, but when I reached out to help myself he snapped his teeth as though he meant to bite my hand off. I quickly learned that it was his place to eat first, then Maman Rita would take her turn, and then I, no longer a privileged puppy but the lowest in rank, was allowed to help myself to the leftovers. No matter; there was usually enough for all.

I shared my purloined meals with them, too. They weren't interested in vegetables, of course, but were quite fond of ham. One evening after we had polished off a hock apiece, we lay stretched out and completely relaxed, digesting happily, in the little clearing at the top of the knoll. After a while we all three felt the urge to amble down the hill to the nearby water hole to have a long drink.

The little pond was a dark mirror, with floating platters of water lilies and spikes of irises along its mossy bank. The wolves dipped their tongues into the cool water and lapped contentedly and I lowered my head and followed their example, lapping with my tongue too. Wrapped in twilight, a wolf on either side of me, I was briming over with pleasure and smiled down to my toes.

But our day wasn't over. Once they had their paws in the water the wolves decided it was bath time. They waded in and swam around a few feet from shore and I joined them, dog-paddling along as I had learned to do with Rita and Ita in Grandfather's pond. At one point a school of little silver fish appeared and the two wolves became very excited and began diving for them, splashing water in all directions. Though it was second nature to me to be silent in the forest, I couldn't hold back my laughter as they ducked underwater again and again, jaws snapping, and emerged loudly snorting water from their nostrils and shaking their heads to empty their ears.

After a few minutes the wolves tired of the sport and waded back to the shore. There they dried themselves by shaking vigorously in stages, from their dripping ears down to their saturated tails, drenching me in the process. I followed suit, taking off my clothes and wringing them as dry as I could. I had to put them back on to discourage mosquitoes on the way back, but as the night was warm I didn't mind being damp.

By the time we returned to the knoll the moon had risen, the stars were glimmering in the deep purple sky and the creatures of the night were chorusing their hearts out.

Their music always put my mind at ease. This evening was too beautiful to sleep away. I sat with my chin on my knees and thought about my parents. Not since my mother's arms cradled me had I felt such peace. Even then, though, I was not safe. I surely had heard my mother's heart beat with fear when I was in her womb. And when I arrived in the world, my mother had swaddled me in fear. Never in my short life had I been a child, carefree and happy in a protective world. The murderous specter of hatred had hung over every minute of my eight years. I was old already when my parents were taken; I was much, much older now.

The only time I felt like a child was when I was with my animal friends. Bathing with the wolves I had not a care in the world. Sitting in the darkness, the wolves resting peacefully nearby, I breathed a deep sigh of relaxation.

Suddenly, beside me Ita began a deep low moan: "Aaaaaaah..." I could feel the hair on the back of my neck stand up with excitement. The sound continued, "aaaaaaah..." growing louder and ascending the scale, then "Oooooooooo..." Ita's song sailed out into the darkness and hovered over the forest, no doubt disturbing all—those creatures sleeping peacefully and those vigilantly awake. As the cry trailed off, Maman Rita lifted her head and broke into a refrain in another key, "Aaaaah-Ooooooo" and her voice followed Ita's into the night. Then Ita began again in still another key.

I lifted my head, cupped my hands to my mouth and let out my own cry, "Aaaah-Ooooo" in my own key. We three continued howling for a minute or more. Then the wolves abruptly stood up, meandered to their sleeping quarters and curled up next to each other. I pulled my oilcloth close to them and drifted off to sleep.

In all my travels the only times I ever slept deeply was when I was with wolves. To this day, even in the safety of my own bed, I sleep "with one eye open," ready to leap up at any unfamiliar noise.

The two wolves acted like teenagers in love. Ita was big and handsome and he carried himself like a leader, with his proud banner of a tail held high in the air. Mama Rita clearly adored him. She would often crouch under his chin, lift her head and tenderly lick his muzzle. Sometimes they would lie side by side, their bodies touching, mouthing each other's snouts and rubbing their faces together affectionately. Wolves, as anyone who is familiar with them knows, are capable of smiling, and these two smiled constantly.

With Ita around, Mama Rita lost her painfully gaunt appearance and we all had enough to eat. We were a family of three and we stuck together and shared everything. I don't ever remember being hungry in the company of those wolves.

By now the pair had become inseparable and always went off together to hunt. If they were in the mood they might allow me to accompany them for a while. We would all three start off, the animals in a sociable frame of mind, staying by my heels, even nudging my legs with their shoulders in a friendly way, grinning their wolfy grins. Then they would begin to cover ground in earnest. When I couldn't keep up Mama Rita would look back several times, then become impatient and grab me by my sleeve or trousers and pull me along like a puppy, until she finally gave up on me. Setting me loose with a few tender licks, she would turn and follow Ita into the woods in search of dinner.

When the wolves engaged in serious travel they had a highly efficient gait. Their spines stayed parallel to the ground, with no bobbing up and down, while their big paws trotted smartly, propelling them along at a surprising speed. They seemed to be gliding on an unseen current rather than walking. When they hit that stride I soon was left behind, no matter how hard I tried to keep up. Then they would veer off on their own course, leaving me alone on the trail. They couldn't stay with me for long; they had more important matters to attend to.

One evening I watched the two of them head out together on a hunt, but the next day, to my surprise, Maman Rita returned alone. Ita didn't show up the following day—nor ever again. I knew them well enough to understand that he wouldn't have left her and gone off by himself. Then I remembered hearing gunshots in the distance earlier that day. Some hunter must have shot him, I realized with dismay.

Maman Rita was not herself. She lay on the ground and hardly raised her head when I spoke to her. Her eyes were troubled and her mood seemed to swing between listlessness and agitation. I could tell she was grieving and I wanted to be able to help her. I nuzzled against her and repeated over and over that I loved her, but what more could I do to console her? Still she stayed close to me the next day and the next, hardly leaving my side for more than a few minutes, as though she found comfort in my company.

Or perhaps she was afraid of losing me too. A few days later I was sleeping soundly when suddenly I was jerked awake and roughly dragged by my jacket through brambles and brush to be set down many yards from our sleeping place. Maman Rita was so forceful I thought she would break my arm. The next morning I realized that I was badly scratched on my face and wherever else my skin was exposed. What had alarmed her? A bear? A human? I never knew, but years later I learned that those woods were full of bounty hunters who, in exchange for a ration of salt, would capture and turn over fugitive Jews to be executed.

We two were on our own again, and our routine began to return to the way it had been before Ita's arrival. One afternoon I was walking alone beside a broad field in which a flock of crows was arguing over carrion. Suddenly: another shot—this time louder and much nearer than before—and in a second the birds levitated into the tops of the trees. A while later I saw a peasant head across a field dragging behind him something tied with a rope—a gray wolf.

No! I couldn't believe it! I stood there a moment, stunned, unable to grasp what had happened. Then rage began to boil up inside me until I was trembling all over. That man, that criminal walking so calmly as if out for an innocent stroll, had killed Maman Rita. Without thinking, I began to follow him, keeping well back and out of sight, as he headed down a lane and across a field. When he reached the other side of the pasture he came to a ramshackle wooden house. There in the yard he dropped the corpse on the ground, leaned his rifle against the wall and went inside.

Crouching in the tall grass, I watched and waited. In a few minutes the hunter came out, an unlit pipe in his mouth. He tightened the rope around my beautiful friend's hind legs and roughly lugged her to the side of the house where he heaved her up and hung her upside down on a hook on the wall. Then he came around to the front of the shack and sat down in a chair near the door. He fumbled for a match in his jacket pocket, lit up his pipe, tilted his chair, and blew out a long stream of smoke. For a while I watched him taking his ease, while Maman Rita's limp body, so strange, so defeated, hung lifeless on his wall.

A surge of terrible rage was burning hotter and hotter in my chest. "Murderer! Murderer!" I screamed silently. "Murderer!" I rose to my feet without thought, without intent, and made my way silently, stealthily around to the rear of the shack.

The back yard was littered with refuse of all kinds—rotting boards, a rusty pail, bent wagon wheels. There, lying on the ground, nearly covered by weeds was a length of heavy metal pipe. I picked it up in both hands and crept around to the front of the house.

The man in the chair had his eyes closed now, his boots off and his feet resting on an overturned wooden bucket. Before he knew what was happening, I had raised the pipe high over my head and smashed it down with all my strength on his knees. His head jerked forward and he shrieked in pain. I raised the pipe again and he lunged at me, clutching at my arms, trying desperately to make me stop. But there was no way I could stop. I struck him again and again.

Finally, when he lay inert and groaning on the ground, I turned away. I stumbled to the rifle, grabbed it, marched straight to the well and threw it in. Then I went around to the side of the house. Maman Rita hung there without dignity, eviscerated, like a chicken in the butcher's window. I lifted her from the hook and set her gently on the ground. With my knife I cut the rope that bound her back legs, then I lifted her as high as I could over my shoulder and half carried, half dragged her back into the woods.

With tears streaming down my cheeks, I bore her proud body down the path she and I had walked just the day before. Coming to a small clearing filled with feathery ferns I gently laid her down. With both hands I dug the soft earth under a pine tree until I had made a shallow hollow, like the one I slept in each night. Then I gently set my friend in her bed, kissed the soft muzzle that had so many times comforted me, and covered her with earth, pine needles and leaves. Not wanting to let her go, I scooped up dirt from the grave and rubbed it on my face and into my hair. Then, kneeling there by the mound, I doubled over in a contraction of grief and wailed. For the second time in my short life, my heart was broken.

I would meet other wolves in my long journey but none could make up for the loss of Maman Rita.

For many days after, I wandered around the forest in a stupor, without eating, without planning, completely bereft of all but my sorrow. The killing of Mama Rita and the disappearance of my own mother and father melded into one and the same loss. How long had it been since my parents disappeared? It seemed like an eternity. Now orphaned for the second time, I felt utterly alone in a cruel and mindless universe.

When I finally came back from the distant realm of my grief, I was truly lost, with no idea of where I was or where I should be going. With Maman Rita gone, the only thing left for me was to resume the search for my parents. But if I hadn't found them by now, what hope was there? East had taken me to Germany where I had believed I might find them, but I had left Germany with no clue to their whereabouts. East had brought me to Poland, with still no trace of my parents. And everywhere I had seen the signs of hatred. I was like the wolves, a hunted animal, one that would be killed on sight. The woods stretched on and on. Not having any reason to stop, I continued to do what I had been doing since the day I ran away—trudge eastward. Hope or no hope, I began following railroad tracks that headed toward the sunrise.

I was lying on the ground, studying the whorls of wide, pointy leaves surrounding stems of little white bells—lilies of the valley. Their sweet, delicate fragrance always reminded me of my mother. For the hundredth time that day I thought of her. Now I tried to remember every detail about her. My mother had a dress I loved—an ivory-colored one with red polka dots. It was made of very soft fabric and was old and worn, but always clean. It had a little attached vest and a skirt that flared at the bottom. She looked so pretty in that dress, with her straight dark hair pulled back in a low ponytail. And I remembered her long slender fingers, like a pianist's, and her ears, small and delicate. Grandfather told me I had ears like hers.

What did she think? What did she feel? My mother believed in God, I knew, because she told me God watches over us from above. Sometimes when she and I were alone together in our dark apartment she would light candles and ask me to pray with her. And I would think, "Why should I pray? God hasn't done much for us lately."

Even then I had a deep sense of injustice. Other children played outside in the sunshine, in beautiful parks full of trees and birds; they could laugh out loud, clap their hands and sing noisily; other children had toys, other children had friends.

My parents told me the Nazis wanted to kill us because we were Jews. That's why we subsisted as fugitives. I was a prisoner in our miserable little flat. I had to stay inside and keep my voice down to a whisper. An energetic, curious child, I almost went crazy with boredom. I never in my life had a friend because we couldn't let anyone find out the truth about us—we were Jews.

On the ground nearby swarmed hundreds of ants, coming and going in the most purposeful way. I lay on my stomach, propped on my elbows and looked down on their nest. "I can wreak havoc on you any time I choose," I said to them. "No matter how hard you work to build your orderly little world, I can crush you all in an instant."

I thought about the God my mother told me about. She taught me that God is cruel only to cruel people. But that didn't make sense. The Nazis were cruel, but God was not cruel to them. On their belts they wore the inscription "*Gott mit Uns*"—God Is with Us.

How could that be?

On the other hand, I am kind. I have always respected every living creature. I would never harm even the ants. Since God spares the cruel Nazis, God in his righteousness should certainly spare me.

But what does God care of righteousness? God turned his face away when my parents were taken by the Nazis, their one mistake, being Jews. And as if that weren't enough, where was God looking when my beautiful mother wolf was killed?

After her death I felt I was dying too, and I retreated from the world and hid in the farthest corner of darkness. Day and night, sunrise and sunset, came and went, measured and unchanged, and I continued to hide away. Yet, somehow, I was still part of the world, and though my trust in God died, I did not. With the passing of time, in my chrysalis of pain, I evolved into another form, hard as steel and full of anger against God.

I studied the ants. We are just God's ants, I reasoned, and He is as cruel and crazy as man. And man—how could I forgive what my child's eyes had witnessed of man? How could I be a human? Transformed by injustice, I was reborn in a form I understood and respected. No longer human, I became in my heart an animal, a wolf. I remember that my lips curled up on my teeth in hatred at the thought of humans.

Recently, now so many years after the war, I was watching my new kitten play with a mouse he had just caught. I discovered Volodia in the basement batting and mauling the tiny rodent. Ordinarily I would have rescued it and set it free outside, but this time I watched for a minute to see if he knew what to do with it. When the mouse tried to get away Volodia would let him run a few inches, then pounce on him again and again. I stepped in and stopped the activity before the mouse got hurt, but later I began thinking about Volodia and his mouse. Some people say behavior such as his shows cruelty, but I disagree. My kitten is just practicing the hunting skills that would enable him to survive in the wild. He means the mouse no harm and he takes no pleasure in its suffering—he doesn't even realize that it is suffering.

I have heard people use the word "bestial" to describe what the Nazis did to their victims; I have heard them say the Nazis "acted like animals." When I hear that I answer, "No, the Nazis acted like humans." Only humans have the capacity to kill for pleasure. Only humans have the capacity to enjoy another's suffering. What I saw the Nazis do to their own kind, no animal has ever done.

I was going along a deer path in the woods, one that more or less paralleled the railroad tracks. The air was moist and smelled of rotting leaves and mushrooms. Today I was fortunate to have company on my walk. I'd met two large, yellow dogs early in the morning and they had traveled with me the whole day. Now they walked by my side or bounded on ahead to scout the territory. Occasionally I stopped to rest and they lay down by my side. I scratched their ears and bellies and offered them something to eat; they responded with gratitude and slobbery kisses. Then we got up and set off again.

At one point, one of the dogs veered off to the side of the path, so I stopped to see what he was up to. He was down on his front elbows with his head under a bush and his hindquarters in the air, sniffing at something I could not see. He came running back to us, whining in agitation, and then returned to the bush where he began a high-pitched yelping.

Curious, I wandered over for a look, the other dog following at my heels. Something was in the leaves there, just the other side of the brush. The dogs were sniffing furiously right beside me as I bent down and pushed the branches aside to see what they'd found.

There in the leaves it lay—a body in a torn, white shirt. I was unprepared for the horrible mutilation I beheld: a bloody swastika carved between the shoulder blades. The gashes were crusty with dried blood and the skin peeled back to expose raw, red muscle tissue beneath. Numb with shock, I eased the figure over on its back and discovered the pale, handsome face of a young man and another horror—a Star of David gouged into his chest. Could someone so disfigured still be alive? I reached for his hand to see if there were any warmth there.

Just then one of the dogs, and then the other, began gently licking the terrible wounds. In a moment I was amazed to see the young man's eyelids flutter open and his gaze slowly turn in my direction. His lips barely moved as he struggled for words, but his eyes spoke to me imploringly. I leaned over him, my ear close to his lips and listened intently.

When he tried again I realized he was speaking Polish. I sat back, shook my head and shrugged to let him know I didn't understand. He tried another language I couldn't make out, and then, "*Français?*" I nodded "yes." His eyes closed again and there followed a long silence. I thought he might be sleeping but still I squatted beside him, watching, waiting. His face was so pale, like a candle, with fine blue veins at the temples, and his dark lashes rested on purple bruises under his eyes. Soft, dark hair, like a child's, curled over his forehead.

In a few minutes he opened his eyes again and whispered something. I shook my head "yes," I was listening. His lips moved again, his voice almost inaudible; he seemed to want to tell me something terribly important. I strained every muscle in my body to hear. The words I remember now can't be exactly what he uttered that day, but they express what he meant. With a great effort he began to tell me his story. He said:

"Listen, please. You must listen. I can't speak long. My name is Marek. I'm an interpreter. The SS, the ones with death heads on their helmets, came to my house at night. They were celebrating. They would have some fun with Jews. Ten or twelve of us were taken at gun point to a warehouse, where they bound and gagged us. They called us "pigs" and "filthy Jews" and beat us...burned us with their cigarettes...carved our flesh with razors. They were all laughing; it was a big joke. When we could hardly stand, they untied us...dragged us into a truck.

"They drove us to these woods, and threw us out of the truck. One of them said, 'All right, now run away. You're free.' I could hardly walk, but I tried to run with the others. The soldiers began shooting at us. I don't know how many were killed. I was too weak to run so I just stood and took a bullet in my shoulder. They left me here for dead. I might have survived the bullet, but I was almost gone anyway. It's over for me."

With great effort he lifted one long, pale hand and placed it softly on mine. "Little mother, remember what you have seen and heard here today. Do not forget. Never forget."

Marek was dying. He had told me so but I would have known anyway. I sat beside him, trying to absorb what he had said, trying to understand the meaning of it all. He was a stranger, this tortured man; we had no history together. Yet how important it was for him to tell someone—to tell me, as it happened—what unspeakable harm had befallen him, before he was silenced forever. And how important it was for me to try to grasp every word.

The forest was still. Marek seemed to be resting quietly after his great exertion. The dogs were lying a few feet away, alert, watchful, their ears pricked up, their eyes troubled. Marek's eyes were closed, his breathing slow and shallow. I sat beside him in silence for a long while, watching his disfigured chest rising and falling almost imperceptibly, the bloody Star of David, transfigured into this hideous form, our common bond.

There was no bird song, no buzzing of insects. I stared at little dabs of sunlight moving back and forth on the ground; an unfelt breeze was stirring the tops of the trees.

Suddenly, in unison, the two dogs got to their feet, as if at a signal. I looked over at them without speaking. Their ears were laid back, their heads down, their tails tucked between their legs. Together they turned and, without glancing at me or Marek, began slowly to move away from the little clearing. When they had gone a short distance, one looked back over his shoulder and our eyes met for an instant. What was in that look? Then he turned his head away and followed his companion into the woods.

My attention returned to Marek. He seemed to have gotten smaller, to have collapsed from the inside. I leaned forward to see into his eyes. They were unfocused and sunken deep into his cheekbones. I wanted to touch him but my palms were callused and rough, so I brushed the back of my hand against his cheek. No response. The dogs had known it: Marek was gone.

I thought of Maman Rita and the earth I'd put over her. Once again it was my duty to make a grave. I gathered up pine needles and leaves and spread them over Marek's sad, broken body, covering every trace of blood. Some day I would bear witness to what I had seen here this day.

For now I began walking again.

The morning air was warm; a pale sun shone thinly through the whitewashed sky. I was off course again, heading north in order to stay within the protection of the forest.

I was tired, tired of dragging myself through swamps and thorn bushes and burnt fields, tired of being cold and wet, tired of hiding. In the villages signs of the German occupation were everywhere—Nazi flags, military vehicles, soldiers on the street acting the part of the conquerors. Consequently, I avoided villages. Whenever I saw that red and white flag with the evil black cross, the blood in my veins turned to ice and I fled in the opposite direction. But the farms were devastated, too. Everywhere I saw deprivation, poverty and misery. I had no choice but to push on and hope for something better ahead.

The trail was narrow and winding and up ahead something unusual caught my eye—a heap of ashes surrounded by rocks. Who had been there? Where were they now?

Cautiously, I crossed the clearing and felt the campfire: cold. I looked around in every direction: nothing. Who could have left this fire? Well, whoever it was had come and gone; I breathed a bit easier.

Back on the trail, the weather was favorable for covering a lot of ground. Several hours later I had forgotten all about the campfire in the clearing. I was walking along the trail when, just a few feet in front of me, a man suddenly stepped from the brush and blocked my way. His hair and beard were wild and he held a pitchfork raised over his head as if he were about to strike me.

Instantly I swerved around to run the other way, but was stopped short by two men blocking the path behind me. My hand went to the dagger in my pocket but I knew I was caught.

The men encircled me and began asking questions in

Polish and I responded with my usual gestures, trying not to show how terrified I was. Then the one with the pitch-fork gripped my wrist and began steering me ahead on the path, the others following behind, while I kept telling myself to keep calm.

We turned off the trail and cut through heavy brush until we came at last to a clearing. Around a crude lean-to made of saplings and evergreen boughs sat a group of men dressed in shapeless caps, frayed jackets, baggy trousers and rags on their feet for shoes. Two or three of the men sported shabby uniforms—not German, I noted with relief. They looked like the Polish peasants I'd seen all over the region. (Much later I learned that this probably was one of the many groups of Polish partisans, members of a loosely knit underground, waging guerrilla warfare against the German occupation.)

After a moment I noticed there were a several women in the group and two or three children—an encouraging sign. Since they had children with them, I reasoned, per-haps they wouldn't harm a child like me.

My captors led me toward a group of men who were seated on the ground, cleaning and loading rifles. A tall man with an angular, pockmarked face stood up and came toward us. He was someone important, I guessed, because the men were explaining about me, perhaps asking him what to do with me. They called him Janusz.

As they spoke this Janusz person looked me over. Then he bent down to peer into my face and said something to me that I didn't understand. I responded by raising my eyes and smiling a sweet, harmless, little girl smile. He stood up, shrugged his shoulders, growled something dismissive to the man with the pitchfork and went back to cleaning his gun. The pitchfork man gestured for me to sit down near the rest of the group, and then he also lost interest in me.

For a while I thought they were going to forget about me and I would be able to slip away. I sat quietly waiting until everyone was busy with their own activities, then stood up and, as casually as I could, began to wander slowly toward the edge of the clearing. I had taken only a few steps when one of the men shouted at me. I turned around and saw the pitchfork man on his feet, ready to pounce, so I ambled back to my spot and sat down as if I'd just been stretching my legs. I stayed there, not moving, but watching carefully.

The afternoon passed quietly. When dusk fell the women gathered wood and started a fire. From a metal rod they suspended a big iron pot and soon I could smell cabbage cooking. In the more than two years I'd been wandering, I'd never had a fire, much less cooked anything. I watched with fascination. When dinner was ready, the members of the group went to the pot and helped themselves, then sat in a circle around the fire and drank from their bowls.

Then one of the women beckoned me over and ladled out a bowl of grayish broth with chunks of vegetables. It didn't taste good, but, unlike the food in my knapsack—unlike everything I'd been eating—it was hot.

Well into the evening the group continued to sit around the fire, the adults murmuring in low tones and passing around a bottle of water. The children drank too. When, it

came my way I took a big swig, swallowed and then—
Ayyyy! Liquid fire! My throat contracted and I was overcome with a coughing spasm that nearly knocked me to the
ground. The people around the fire turned and laughed.
This colorless fluid wasn't water but a fierce moonshine
vodka called "bimber." To those accustomed to it, no doubt
it was useful for warming the gut on cold nights and soft-
ening the edges of anxiety, but it was too much for me.

An owl hooted, the embers of the cooking fire flickered
and faded and the children lay with their heads in their
mothers' laps. Curled up on my oilcloth under a tree a few
feet away, I felt uneasy, distressed to be so close to people.
Occasionally one of the children would look over at me
curiously and I looked back, but neither of us moved from
our places.

As the hour grew late members of the group disappeared into the branch hut, their sleeping quarters. I stayed
awake listening to the growls and screams of a polecat and
thinking I would be able to sneak away once the last stragglers dozed off, but all through the night the men took
turns as sentries, sitting in the clearing, their rifles across
their knees. Everyone seemed somber and on edge. Feeling
the same, I got little sleep.

The next morning no one prepared any kind of breakfast. As I huddled there, tired and miserable, Janusz, the
leader, began barking orders and rounding up members of
the group. One of the men motioned to me, so I joined
them, feeling awkward and out of place.

We set off through the woods in single file, sticking
close together along the narrow path. They placed me in

the middle of the group, no doubt because of my attempted escape. I kept pace with them, trying not to do anything to draw attention to myself and wishing myself a thousand miles away.

Janusz, his rifle on his shoulder, led the party and several other armed men with rows of bullets in their belts followed him closely. We trudged along for a while until the woods ended and we arrived at a wide dirt road with high brush on either side. Janusz waved his hand signaling everyone to crouch down in the bushes beside the road. I squatted down too and we all waited. The men kept looking into the distance as if expecting something or someone important, but I had no idea what or who it was.

After what seemed like hours I heard the hum of a car motor in the distance, growing louder. As the vehicle came abreast of where we were hiding, Janusz suddenly rose and hurled something into the road. There was a loud explosion followed by a huge cloud of white smoke. I heard a squeal of brakes, then shouts. Janusz and the armed men ran out to the road with the others close behind them. Through the trees I could see a green military car, with a chauffeur in front and a German officer in the back seat, pulled off to the side of the road. Janusz held his rifle on the driver, while two others aimed at the officer in the back.

With the barrel of his gun Janusz motioned the driver to get out of the car. The man opened the door and came out slowly, his hands above his head. I heard him demand something in an indignant, imperious voice. Janusz answered by spinning him around and shoving him to his knees in the road. Then he took aim and fired a single shot.

The man's head snapped back convulsively and he collapsed face down. A syrup of blood oozed from his temple and pooled on the packed earth.

Janusz's men opened the rear door of the car and dragged the officer in back out into the road. With a crack to the face, one of them knocked the German back against the car. The other one immediately fired two rapid shots into the officer's tight fitting, smartly buttoned jacket and he slid down the side of the car, leaving a smear of blood on the shiny fender. His visored cap askew, his gleaming high boots outstretched, the once formidable commander of Hitler's finest lay like a broken scarecrow against the rear tire. The man with the pitchfork who had been standing behind me suddenly ran up and plunged the tines deep into the officer's throat.

I watched intently, not because I liked what I saw—it was disgusting, in fact—but because I was fascinated by the sheer horror of it all. Does that seem strange? It is human nature—I was acting just like any passing driver who slows down at the scene of a horrible accident, hoping to catch a glimpse of the carnage.

Janusz beckoned to one of the children, a boy about 13 or 14, who rolled the bleeding man over, then held a feather under his nose. I didn't realize until later that they wanted to see if the man was breathing. Perhaps he was, because Janusz put a final bullet through his skull, then confiscated the victim's gun and bullets, removed his watch and went through all his pockets.

Several of the partisans quickly stripped the bodies naked, stashed the clothing and boots in their packs and dragged the bloody corpses into the woods, as others searched the automobile. Then they pushed the vehicle off the road into the brush, and the children were sent out, each with a leafy branch, to brush dirt over the scorched and bloody road and throw the victims' hats into the woods. As we left, I looked back over my shoulder—there was no sign of the violent scene that had occurred just moments before on that deserted stretch of road.

That night I was so exhausted I fell asleep immediately, but my sleep was troubled by terrifying nightmares. In the middle of the night I dreamed I was being chased by a man with a knife. I was running as fast as I could but he kept gaining on me. Suddenly he grabbed me! I felt the blade against my back and tried desperately to scream, but nothing came out. I awoke with sweat pouring off me, my arms and legs thrashing, and heard myself utter a whispered, "No!" The dream was so real I couldn't go back to sleep and I lay awake for hours waiting for dawn.

The next day, preparations began again for another foray. The men took up their weapons, and Janusz distributed hand grenades to several of them. Then we all set out, marching down another trail to the end of the woods and a different road, and once again waited in the brush. After a while, a military convoy comprised of dozens of vehicles marked with black swastikas passed by, but we all stayed in our places. Too large a target, I surmised.

Much later, a single automobile approached. Janusz and his men rose quickly from the brush and crept closer to the edge of the road. In their hands some held grenades. The car came nearer and I could see it was a large open one, shiny green, with smartly uniformed German officers front and back. Just then, Janusz gave the signal and his men pulled the pins from their grenades and hurled them with deadly accuracy into the open vehicle. The auto screeched and swerved, there were shouts of alarm, then a deafening explosion. An orange fireball rose into the sky followed by billowing clouds of black smoke. The partisans gave a cheer but remained in the woods. Tiny particles of ash rained down around us.

When the fire had subsided, several of the partisans went out and dragged the charred bodies from the car and pitched them into the woods. Others pushed the smoldering car into the ditch and covered it with branches. One of the women came up to me and handed me a branch and I understood I was to join the children in sweeping the evidence from the road. I complied by brushing away the charred dirt, tossing into the bushes whatever I found—a door handle, the visor of a soldier's cap, wires, fragments of debris too burnt to identify. One of the older boys picked up an object and began waving it around like a boomerang. It was part of an arm.

Later that day, back at camp, two members of the troop arrived with a sack of vegetables—half rotten potatoes, onions and cabbages—and the women began preparing dinner. When it was done they beckoned me over. Even the terrible scene I had witnessed could not stay my hunger, but I took no pleasure in sharing their meal with them.

I don't remember how many days I spent with those people—three or four, maybe more, though it was an eternity at the time. One morning, I sat on my oilcloth thinking,

"I can't go out with them again." I was sick of the killing. But when the group was ready to leave one man came over and lifted me up by my arms and I knew I had no choice. They weren't going to leave me behind. Although I was only a little girl, they understood that a child could give them up as quickly as an adult.

As the men were strapping on their weapons there suddenly came a distant but clear whistle. Everyone stopped what they were doing and listened. The whistle came again. It was a warning, an alert. Suddenly, fear was everywhere. The entire party frantically gathered up their belongings and began running down the path away from the road. I immediately grabbed my knapsack and jacket and rushed after them—or pretended to. As soon as we were in the woods, I veered off in another direction. Either they didn't notice my departure or were too much in a hurry to care, but I was finally free of them and on my own again.

Like partisans in other occupied countries, many of the Polish guerrillas hid out in the woods where the Germans were least likely to venture.

Their hatred of the Nazis, however, was not necessarily a sign that they supported the Jews. In fact, some groups hated Jews as much as they did Germans, while others accepted Jews and, at times, even collaborated with Jewish partisan groups. I have no idea which was the case with the ones who captured me, but I always was glad I didn't open my mouth and perhaps expose myself to more danger.

Poland
Summer 1942

I BEGAN WATCHING THEM THROUGH THE TREES—seventy-five to a hundred of them. Many looked as if they could hardly hold themselves up, let alone walk. They didn't talk, didn't even look at each other, just plodded ahead in a long ragged line.

Some carried suitcases. Others were pulling small wagons piled high with boxes and bags or pushing baby carriages crammed with everything but babies. Some had huge bundles slung over bent backs—bed sheets stuffed with all their worldly belongings. There were old people shuffling along with canes, gaunt teenagers wheeling bikes, weary mothers with infants in their arms; I wondered how they could nurse their babies and still stay with the crowd.

Each of them wore a yellow emblem. I remembered the six-pointed Jewish star in the center of a brass candleholder my parents had. That was the *menorah* with nine candles that we only took out of hiding for the Hanukah festival—happy times for us.

A rush of excitement came over me. Could my own mother and father be somewhere in that group of Jews going by, so close to where I was standing? I scrutinized each and every adult who passed me, my heart beating faster. Wait—that woman near the end of the line, with the dark hair? She was the right height, she walked just like my mother. Joy overtook excitement but as the woman came closer, my heart plummeted; she looked nothing at all like Maman.

I started to head back to my trail in the woods when the idea occurred to me that perhaps those marchers were heading someplace where the Germans were holding Jewish prisoners and so perhaps they could eventually lead me to Maman and Papa. I decided to follow along.

As the last stragglers went by, I stepped out into the road and began walking behind them, keeping my eyes fixed on the ground, not looking right or left. Jewish or not, I wanted no discourse with them, no questions. In any case there was little chance of that. Nobody said a word to me, as if I were invisible.

We walked on past the end of the woods, past parched meadows, crumbling farmhouses, abandoned grist mills and fields blackened by fire, where only weeds sprouted from the scorched earth. We kept to the middle of the road, moving to the edge when necessary to make room for a passing truck or a hay wagon.

The dust raised by the procession was so thick at the end of the line that it clogged my nostrils and ground into my eyes. We must have trudged along for hours on that road with no shade. The scorching sun directly overhead made the blood pound in my temples. My throat was so dry that when I saw a boy ahead of me lift a glass jar to his lips and drink, I almost fainted with longing.

Just when I thought I couldn't take another step, we came to a small village with a tiny square and a public well. Everyone rushed up to the water pump and took turns jerking the handle and letting spurts of water from the spigot splash into their mouths and over their faces. As I stood in line waiting impatiently for my turn I spotted a thin, ragged jacket lying in the dust on the ground. When I held it up, I saw on the sleeve a band with a yellow star crudely stitched in black thread. I turned it inside out to hide the emblem and tied it around my waist—I would never pass up an opportunity to acquire an item of clothing.

The line resumed its march and eventually we came to a more populated area. The houses were closer together now, and there were street vendors, a blacksmith, a tannery, a school and several churches. We turned onto a street paved with cobblestones and I saw a sign with a word I immediately recognized: "Warszawa." The spelling, though different from what I'd seen on Grandfather's map, was close enough to tell me that we were in Warsaw.

I was plodding numbly ahead when suddenly a woman beside me cried out and fell to the ground, bleeding from a gash under her eye. I turned and saw at the side of the road two teenagers hurling rocks and jeering. The woman pulled herself to her feet as the parade of misery flowed past her, continuing its staggered progress through the city of Warsaw. I worried that we would encounter more rock throwers but we did not, although once in a while, as we wound our way along the thoroughfares, someone would turn and stare at us or shout something. Mostly, though, we were ignored. Apparently, such a sorry group as ourselves was not an unusual sight for these urban residents.

Passing through grimy neighborhoods where decay and neglect bore dreary testimony to the effects of war, we came upon whole bombed out, skeletonized city blocks where children scampered over shards of broken glass and grotesquely twisted, rusty pipes and played hide-and-seek amid immense piles of rubble. As the afternoon progressed the lowering sun shone incongruously outward from windows of buildings whose front wall had remained standing when the rest of the edifice was leveled to the ground.

We passed out of that architectural bone yard and into a squalid, congested neighborhood of low tenements. There, an air of expectation arose as people in the line began to murmur and point. I guessed we had arrived somewhere important, perhaps our destination, when two armed German soldiers in helmets and high boots appeared at the head of the line and began checking the marchers one by one, inspecting their papers and marking them on a list. Suddenly, panic gripped me. Was I supposed to show papers too? I didn't have any!

I looked around for a way to avoid meeting up with those soldiers. Nearby a group of neighborhood children were playing jacks on the sidewalk. Slowly I began to inch my way through the marchers toward them, pausing if anyone seemed to be looking in my direction. I separated myself from the group, ambled to the side of the street and sat down on a stoop near the other children, where I pretended to be playing with a pile of pebbles. No one showed any interest in me. I was able to slip into an alley and hide there until the crowd moved on. When the last of the marchers was almost out of sight I emerged and began following them again, but this time at a greater distance.

The procession eventually came to a gray brick wall and halted. I had no way of knowing that this barrier enclosed the notorious Warsaw Ghetto. As the marchers stood waiting by an entrance it was impossible not to notice the nauseating stench that hung heavily in the air. I reentered the alley and worked my way through back yards, emerging near the head of the line. Peering from a gateway I saw that the helmeted soldiers were talking to guards in blue uniforms stationed by the iron gate. I sat down in the dust to watch. What I observed next I did not understand. A policeman wearing an officer's cap came striding imperiously down the line and began ordering people around in the roughest manner. The weary marchers shuffled from foot to foot but the policeman would not let them sit. On his sleeve this petty tyrant wore an armband with a Jewish star. I didn't get it. This man, apparently a Jew, was dressed like a policeman and behaving like someone in power— why? (After the war I learned about the Jewish police who cooperated with the Germans in exchange for power and privileges or merely in the hope of saving themselves or their loved ones.)

After a long delay the guard opened the gate and everybody waited expectantly. I slipped along the edge of the group to try to see what was inside. The crowd parted and I had a clear view of the open gate framing a city street, like the one I was on, and figures inside wearing armbands. So there were Jews in there! Could my mother and father be there too?

I expected that the marchers would be going through the gate, but the guards closed it after admitting only one soldier, leaving everyone else outside. Much later I wondered if the exhausted marchers meekly waiting by the gate still believed the lies: that they would find a new home in the ghetto, that perhaps they might even be reunited with friends and loved ones who had been deported before them. I have no idea whether they eventually were taken in because I walked on and soon lost sight of them.

How could I get inside the wall to look for my parents? Not through that gate, that was for sure. Even if they opened it again, I had no intention of letting myself be added to their list. I'd climbed over walls many times, but this one looked too high for me—ten feet, at least. Evening was coming and I decided not to attempt to get inside at this late hour. I would hole up for the night and make a plan in the morning.

Next morning when the sun came up, I prowled the backyards looking for something to eat and managed to reach in an open window to snitch a loaf of brown bread. Then I went back to the wall and began following it, to see if there was any unguarded access or some kind of gap or opening to slip through. There was nothing. As I turned and began to walk away I came upon a little boy with a jaunty cap, frayed knickers and no shoes sitting on the curb, puffing on a cigarette. Since I'd had no luck on my own I wondered if he could tell me how I might get inside. As I approached him I tried to think of a way to make myself understood without speaking.

The boy threw his head back and growled something at me in Polish, the cigarette butt clenched in the corner of his mouth, his eyes squinting from the smoke. I didn't want him to know I couldn't understand his language—he might suspect something—so I put a finger to my lips and shook my head "no," to indicate that I couldn't talk. I pointed over the wall, then to myself. The boy shook his head "no," picked up a stick from the ground and began drawing something in the dirt—a Jewish star. He pointed to the star and then to the wall and made a slashing gesture like a knife across his throat.

There was no misunderstanding that! But I had to let him know that even though I got his message, I still wanted to go in to look around for myself. I pointed to my eyes, then to the wall. He looked at me as if I were crazy, but still I kept gesturing imploringly. At last he shrugged his shoulders, snuffed out his cigarette stub with his thumb and motioned for me to follow him.

I stayed close on his heels as he led me to where the wall turned a corner. He stopped short, took a quick, furtive look over his shoulder, nodded toward the bottom of the wall, then casually strolled back toward where I'd found him.

Now what? I looked down at the spot he had indicated. A pile of trash was heaped against the base of the wall. I pushed it aside with my foot and discovered a hole just large enough for someone my size to squeeze through. Standing there staring at it and recalling the boy's neck-slashing gesture, I struggled for the courage to crawl through.

I could not know then that almost everyone inside that gray brick wall was doomed: As part of the "final solution," within a few days or weeks, on July 22, the Nazis would begin the total extermination of the Jews of the Warsaw Ghetto. Nearly all—men, women and children—would be sent from this ghetto to the Treblinka death camp.

I had no idea what I'd be letting myself in for as I walked back and forth along the wall, chiding myself: "And you imagine you're so brave? Suppose Maman is in there? Will you turn your back on her now?" With that thought, I had no choice but to go in.

I went back to the hole. Could I fit? Barely. I lay on my belly and looked through the opening but all I could make out was debris piled on the other side too. When I reached my hand in to clear it away, I saw a deserted alley. I wriggled first my arms and then my shoulders through, and looked around. All clear. I squirmed my legs through, reached back for my knapsack, stood up and peered around. As there was no one in sight I did not realize immediately that I had not merely crawled through a wall—I had descended into hell.

Quickly I stood up and covered the hole with trash, then began cautiously walking toward a main street, hugging the buildings and looking left and right. The thoroughfare was crowded with shabby people, all so desperately thin they looked to be starving to death. I had never seen such human misery. Many had wounds—open sores, boils, swollen eyes, dirty bandages wrapped around some injury, and they smelled terrible, as though they had not bathed in weeks. All were wearing arm bands with yellow stars. I shrank to the side to avoid being noticed, but they passed without even glancing my way as I continued on.

The streets I walked were ugly and depressing. Stolid four- and five-story brick and stucco buildings squatted on their haunches, their indifferent sooty windows flapping grimy curtains, revealing no comfort within. Stone borders that perhaps once enclosed flower beds were weedy and littered with trash; piles of refuse and excrement collected in the gutter. The few trees I encountered stood parched and thin, looking too discouraged to grow. On the corners where streets crossed were the usual shops, but their dark windows displayed no wares, and most were boarded up and abandoned.

The smell that I had noticed outside the wall was much worse now. It was a combination of feces, urine and decomposing flesh. As I continued down the street I came upon a dead man lying right there on the sidewalk. His naked body was barely covered with newspapers; bony white legs protruded on one end and a horrible skull stared out the other. I gasped when I realized what it was and quickly ducked into an open vestibule to assess the situation.

A group of men passed the doorway where I was crouching and I could hear them talking casually in Yiddish, as if there were no cadaver lying there in the street. Another passerby said to her companion in French "When are they going to cart him away?" and the other answered, matter-of-factly "Not till tomorrow morning. They only come in the morning."

What manner of ghastly place was I in where people scarcely noticed a corpse in the middle of the street! But perhaps they wouldn't notice me either, so that was good. I had heard French being spoken, so maybe there were people here from Belgium. I decided to continue walking, keeping my eyes and ears open for anyone who might know about my parents. Whenever I came upon a group of people talking together I sauntered alongside to try to catch a word or two of their conversation. I heard Polish, German and Yiddish, but I did not hear French again that afternoon.

Everywhere, on every corner, I saw beggars, sometimes alone, sometimes huddling together in twos and threes. Above the street, old women and children, their elbows on the window sill, looked down with vacant eyes and grim faces on the milling traffic below. Amid a group of idlers on the corner, an old crone was selling soup. Someone would occasionally hand her a coin and hold out a bowl which she filled from a metal pail. I turned down a side street and then another and encountered more half-dead people with nothing to do, standing around outside vacant shops or clustered on stoops.

Once I saw a pair of uniformed guards patrolling a gate with big black and tan dogs—German shepherds—by their side. I slipped into an ally and hurried off along another route thinking how fortunate I was that the guards were not looking my way. Suddenly I realized that my lack of a star would have aroused suspicion had I been spotted. I untied the jacket around my waist, turned it right side out and quickly put it on.

All that day I continued combing the streets for a familiar face, trying to peer into the hollow eyes I passed without drawing attention to myself. I had come here with high hopes. Even if I did not find my parents, I thought I might at least meet someone from my old neighborhood who could tell me where they were. But I was making no progress. If there were people here who could lead me to Maman and Papa, wretched as they'd be now, I doubted that I'd even recognize them. I couldn't walk up to strangers and ask, "Are you from Belgium?" Even though they were Jews, that fact alone was no reason to trust them.

I turned down an alley, wriggled through a fence and crawled under a back porch to rest in the dank darkness and think. Across the backyards a poignant lament floated from the strings of a violin, a song of longing and despair, wending its way through the ugly streets. I closed my eyes and let it comfort me. Suddenly the music stopped, and in the next moment the air was torn by the wail of a hungry baby.

In late afternoon I turned a corner and came upon a group of children who looked like no children I'd ever seen in my life. They were more dead than alive. One was a skeleton with arms like white twigs and a mask face. He was holding out his hand, begging. Another was lying unmoving on a doorstep; from deep sockets his eyes, cloudy and hopeless, fixed on mine. Another child, perhaps four or five years old, so tiny she looked like a little brown wren, lay crumpled on the sidewalk in a pool of diarrhea, sucking her thumb.

Suddenly it dawned on me: It could happen to me if I stay here. I could end up like them, dying in the street. The voice in my head screamed, "Get out, get out! Go back through the hole. Now!"

But where was the hole? I remembered it wasn't far from a gate, but hadn't I seen other gates in the wall just like the first one? How far had I gone? I stopped in my tracks. At the very next corner two German officers were standing by a goose-necked light post, talking and looking in my direction. In a split second I slipped inside the nearest doorway.

The hallway stank of sweat and urine and was pitch dark except for a crack of light that seeped in between double doors. As I hid there trying to remember the route back, I could hear the floorboards squeaking above and a steady "pitta-pitta-pitta" of a sewing machine. My eye to the gap between the doors, I watched the street, waiting for the right moment to hurry back to freedom.

Outside the street was full of people, shambling along as if they had nowhere to go and were in no hurry to get there. A woman in the crowd caught my attention because she was very obviously pregnant. A German soldier was walking right behind her. Just as she came abreast of where I was hiding she stumbled and fell to the pavement. The soldier stopped abruptly and angrily shouted something at her. As she started to pull herself up, he grabbed her by the neck and shoved her down. People around scattered like pigeons. Again the woman tried to pull herself up and crawl away, but he began kicking her. Sobbing, she tried to cover her swollen belly with her arms. Without warning, the soldier drew his pistol from its holster and shot her neatly in the head, then straightened his jacket and calmly walked away. A group of men sitting nearby on the curb didn't even turn to look at the broken figure bleeding in the gutter.

How could this have happened? I had witnessed it but I couldn't believe it. Would I ever stop trembling? I had to get out of this hideous place immediately, get back to the wall and find the opening. I steadied myself and made my hand push open the door.

With exaggerated nonchalance I slowly strode down the street, then turned the corner and began to hurry, retracing my steps as best I could remember. Several times I lost my way, and I worried that darkness would overtake me before I could find the route that led back to freedom. Then I recognized the landmarks I'd passed when I arrived—that little grocery was the same one I'd seen on the way in and over there was the intersection with an uprooted street light where I'd changed direction. The sun was setting and I began to run. When I spotted the corner of the wall where I had crawled through, I felt a flood of relief. I quickly reached the spot and stopped short.

The hole was sealed with fresh cement.

That night I tried to sleep in a stairwell behind a tenement. As I lay there sweating in the suffocating heat, breathing a stench of rotten fish and human waste and listening for the sound of footsteps coming to get me amid the perpetual wail of children, I thought what a horrible fix I'd gotten myself into. I was in a nightmare but I couldn't wake up. It was impossible to look for my parents here; every step I took led me closer to disaster.

When the pale, gray morning came I began walking along the length of the wall, searching for a way out. I passed by gates patrolled by German soldiers or Jewish police and carefully examined the unguarded sections, hoping to find an opening like the one I had crawled through. No luck; I was trapped.

When I wasn't studying the wall, I tried to keep myself invisible by staying close to groups of street urchins, children like me with no parents to look after them, no bed to sleep in and little or nothing to eat. Once I heard a couple of them speaking French—a boy around ten and a girl with dirty braids, playing some kind of game. The boy was saying to the girl:

"No, I win, I told you—mother and father deported, that's two (he threw two pebbles on the ground); sister died of typhus, that's three (one more pebble down); my brother shot, that's four (down with the fourth pebble). So who've I got left? Me!" He opened his hand triumphantly to show the one pebble left.

That evening I came upon a street I had not seen before. The rows of once gracious buildings had fancy iron balconies and window boxes that must have billowed with flowers in an earlier time. They were empty now, as was a dress shop down the street with a naked mannequin in the window and a boarded up theater, beneath whose blank marquee a faded billboard framed a ballerina in mid-jeté. Amid all this desolation, I spied a restaurant that was open for business, with a sign "*Restauracja*," and ornate gas lights glowing on either side of the entrance. It was like a dream, yet so familiar and normal that it reminded me of the cafés and bistros Marthe and I saw that day in Brussels.

As I walked by, a man and woman came through the front door. He wore a gray suit, and she, a flowery print dress and a pretty hat. Both had armbands with yellow stars on their stylish sleeves. How was it possible that Jewish people could be all dressed up and eating out, right in this hell hole? I later learned that wealthy Jews had been able to buy necessities and even luxuries from the thriving black market, almost up to the time they too were shipped off to the gas chamber.

I went around to the back of the restaurant and found a metal garbage can. Not much inside—others probably had gotten there before me. Still, I scraped up a few shriveled vegetable peels and drank water from a slimey rain barrel—every bit helped.

The third morning just before sunrise I was curled up under a stairway unable to sleep. My loaf of stolen bread was long gone. Though my stomach was empty, the stifling heat and the ungodly stench made me nauseous. What had I gotten myself into? Outside the wall, I had been in danger many times, yes, but outside I was free! Outside I was surrounded by the beauty of my wild kingdom. But here—here I was a caged animal, a rat in a corner, trapped amid death and ugliness, with nowhere to go, no way to get away. My God, I might perish here in this evil place.

As I lay there in a silent panic I heard a rumbling of cartwheels on the cobblestone pavement. Peeking out I saw a wooden wagon like the kind vegetable venders used, pulled by two men and pushed on both sides by two others. In the back, naked, fleshless skeletons with drawn skin and staring eyes were stacked helter-skelter, their heads and limbs lolling with each jerk of the wagon.

Two little boys dressed in rags followed the wagon. I wondered why those two were walking behind. Curiosity? Someone they knew among the dead? Then I had an idea: If the wagon were going to a cemetery outside the gate perhaps I could somehow get out too. Among the many idlers on the street no one paid the slightest bit of attention to the children walking behind, so I decided to follow too.

We had gone but a short distance when we came to an abrupt halt. A corpse had toppled off the wagon and lay sprawled stiffly in the middle of the street. The boys each grabbed an extremity and heaved the creature back on the pile like a bale of hay. I guessed that picking up fallen bodies was their job.

The cart started up and I again began walking behind. We stopped once or twice to collect more bodies then headed into a flat, desolate area of rubble and weeds. I looked ahead and my heart sank. The men were steering the wagon into a cemetery, all right, but it wasn't outside the wall.

The wagon trundled through a pair of imposing iron gates and through the rows of tombstones while I stayed outside, unsure of what to do next. The putrid odor I had been smelling for days was now overwhelming. It wrapped like a shroud around my head and clung to the little hairs in my nostrils and to my tongue; it coated the back of my throat and clung to my clothes. When I held my breath it came in through my eyes and my ears and my hair and my skin.

No matter, no matter, I decided, I was out of options; I had nothing to lose by going in there. Inside the cemetery the men wheeled the cart past long, neat rows of pale, stone slabs with names and dates and messages of devotion from the living, reminders of an earlier time when death came singly, not by the thousands. At last the cart drew up to a gaping pit with mounds of earth piled on two sides. I ducked behind a headstone and waited while the children dragged the bodies down from the cart and threw them, one by one, into the pit.

The job finished, the cart turned around, trundled by me a few feet away, rolled again past the stately marble obelisks and through the rows of white slabs, precise as crops in a field, and out the high iron gates. I watched it until it disappeared from sight and I was left alone with the dead.

The sight and stench of the unburied corpses made me swoon, but hiding among the rotting Jews was safer than being out on the street with the soldiers and police. More important, I could see the wall at the back perimeter of the graveyard. If I could wait there until dark, perhaps I'd come across an opening or some other way to get out.

I climbed to the top of a dirt mound and began digging with my hands. The soil was loose and soon I had a hole large enough to hide myself in. From there I could look out to see anyone entering or leaving the cemetery.

It was early morning but the sun hid behind a wall of clouds and the dull sky looked smeared and chalky. Too terrified to go back to sleep, I closed my eyes, buried my nose in my collar in a vain attempt to escape the smell and tried to rest. The air was so heavy with humidity that my whole body felt wet and clammy and sweat poured down my face.

I hid there all day in the searing heat. Occasionally another cart would roll in to deposit more bodies in the pit and then promptly leave, or a solitary guard would make perfunctory rounds. Buried alive by my own hand I lay without moving until nightfall, with the stench of death seeping into my living cells—I shall carry that smell with me the rest of my life.

Darkness came early, ushered in by ominous roiling clouds and a quick drop in temperature. I was alone in the graveyard. A sodden wind whipped up dust clouds along the tops of the mounds. The sky turned dark green and eerie. Phosphorescent tracer rounds of lightening on the horizon were followed long seconds later by rolls of distant thunder. A few sprinkles fell, dotting the earth that enclosed me.

That was my signal, my green light. The storm, I hoped, would discourage any more visitors that day. As I pulled myself out of the dirt and started to slide down the mound my hand got caught under something hard and gummy—a leg. I pushed it aside and slid to the ground. After brushing myself off and stamping the circulation back into my limbs, I set off for the wall.

The sky was growing black now without a sliver of moon, but I'd long ago become accustomed to maneuvering in darkness. Walking in a crouch with my arms outstretched in front of me, I made my way quickly past the open pits half full of rotting bodies and between toppled gravestones, heading across the cemetery. Then the storm struck in earnest. The pelting downpour drenched my clothes and filled my shoes so they sloshed with each step. Brilliant crackles of light split the black sky, and at times the gales were so strong I had to hunch down on the ground so as not to be blown over.

I arrived at the far wall and began to slide my hands over the wet surface, searching for openings. My eyes filled with rain as I felt my way blindly along, examining every brick within reach, especially the bottom ones. I went carefully, methodically up and down the wall, my fingers seeking, probing, willing the wall to open up a small space for me.

At one point, I discovered a loose brick a few feet off the ground, at the level of my waist. When I pulled, it came out easily. But, to my disappointment, the others next to it were all firmly cemented.

Still I persisted as wind and rain lashed at my face and thunder barreled across the heavens like the devil's own freight train. I pushed my wet hair out of my eyes and with both hands probed again and again, fingering each brick, back and forth, inch by inch along the length of the wall and found—nothing.

For the first time in those terrible days of imprisonment I lost control; my knees buckled and I collapsed in the mud and sobbed. The rain was coming down in sheets now and the wind screamed like a tormented soul in an asylum. Whip cracks of lightening exploded right over my head, followed immediately by deafening claps of thunder.

For a long time I sat in the puddle in the pouring rain, my head bowed. Tears ran down my cheeks mingling with raindrops. Defeated, I would try to find a place to sleep and perhaps make it through one more day. Maybe something would turn up tomorrow—a miracle.

I dragged myself to my feet and slowly began walking toward the back of the cemetery, my heart in my shoes. If I could not find a way to escape, at least my misery would be short. In this hideous place I would be dead soon enough. But if I had to die I only wished I could have died free, beneath the wide heavens, surrounded by a forest and all the wild creatures I had come to love as my friends. If only I could have tasted freedom just once more.

My feet were walking automatically while my mind was far away, in a peaceful forest with my beautiful wolves. As I approached the far corner, I noticed something that broke my train of thought—illuminated by quick, flashbulb pops of lightening I glimpsed a mound, large and dark, on the ground against the wall. More bodies? I walked over cautiously, stopping a few feet away. A long flare of lightening gave me a clear view—no, it wasn't bodies but a low pile of rubble. It might serve as a hiding place for the night. I could bury myself there until dawn. I longed to close my eyes and give myself over to the oblivion of sleep.

Exhausted, I put my hand out and collapsed against the wall. What was this? The rows of bricks were not as smooth and regular as the ones I'd examined before. Feeling the surface with both hands, I discovered a couple of jutting bricks and rough crevices. Could they help me get up that wall? I tried to hook the toe of my shoe on a protruding brick. No good; it was too high.

But now the fever was rising in me again. Frantically, with both hands I began heaping rubble from the mound higher against the wall so that I could stand on it. Finally, my foot reached the irregular brick. Then, with the tips of my fingers, I managed to grab onto a small niche high above me and pull myself off the ground. I lost my hold immediately, however, and couldn't get a firm grasp, though I tried again and again.

My fingers began exploring other areas. Off to one side a square brick column formed part of the wall. It felt rougher than the wall itself. I started over again. By pulling, pushing and gripping with my fingers and toes, taking advantage of tiny crevices and ledges in the bricks, I inched myself half way up. Yes! I was doing it!

I had made it up few inches higher, all the while telling

myself not to panic, not to look down, when suddenly I slipped and landed with a bone-wrenching whack in the mud below. This was hopeless. How could I imagine that I could climb that wall? The rain was letting up, but the lightening continued with enough frequency for me to see the crevices. Fighting back tears, I forced myself to get up and try again.

Suddenly—barking in the distance. Dogs! Did military dogs patrol this wall? The voices of dogs had always comforted me, but now the thought of being torn to bits by vicious teeth struck terror in my heart. I desperately began clawing and groping at the rough surface. This time, this time, I had to make it. Straining with all my will, I secured a toe hold, then a finger hold, then another, and another. Like a human fly, I slipped the bonds of impossibility and, somehow, some way, hooked my fingernails into crumbling mortar, forced my toes into minute indentations, clawed my way higher and higher, got one arm over the top of the wall, pulled with all my might and looked over to—freedom!

A street lamp on the other side beamed its yellow light through the bleary drizzle. Above me, the last obstacle: double rows of barbed wire bolted to a metal post. I clenched my hands around the post then swung my legs over the top of the wall.

To my surprise, getting past the wire was no problem. With my small, thin frame I could easily wriggle under the sharp barbs. I peered down the other side. It was a sheer drop to the cobblestone pavement, wet and gleaming in the lamplight, far below. There was nothing to break my fall. My stomach clenched in a tight knot. Clutching the top of the wall, I slid one leg over the side. Poised there to catch my breath, I suddenly heard barking again—this time louder and closer than before. That did it. I jumped.

I can't recall what happened right after that. Did I black out? I only remember my terror. I was free but not out of danger. If the police found me there, they'd shoot me on the spot. Dazed by my fall and unable to stand, I began crawling away from the lighted street.

The night air was cool after the storm and, once I was out of the light, my head began to clear. I could feel blood trickling down both ankles, but I quickly figured out that I had broken nothing. As soon as I was able to stand, I began walking—hobbling and staggering, actually—down the empty streets, looking for the outskirts of the city.

I limped on and on, desperate to put distance between myself and that hateful wall. After what seemed a very long time I came upon railroad tracks. This would be a good place to stop. In the morning I would follow the rails, but for the moment I couldn't move. I hid myself in the brush and looked around.

Suddenly I realized that I was seeing, in the distance, city lights gleaming across a body of water. Water! Could this be a mirage? I rose unsteadily to my feet and began walking again. When I reached the bank of the river, I waded in, ducked my head into its merciful coolness and drank until I could drink no more. Then I closed my eyes, submerged myself and scrubbed away the smell of death that clung to my hair, skin and clothes. At last I lay on my back in the shallows, soaking my aching legs.

Stretched out there, swept away on a tide of relief, my

mind began working again and I realized that my respite would be short for I'd have to get up and move on, away from the city. Suddenly I found myself desperately longing for woods, for a forest where I could breathe freely again, a stream to drink from and wash my wounds, a bed of soft pine needles and a sweet stray dog to curl up with.

The hole I had used to enter the Warsaw Ghetto had probably been used by a smuggler, a child of perhaps six or seven. Such "runners" would sneak out of the ghetto to beg or steal food for their starving families, then return by the same route. Many such children were caught and shot, sometimes betrayed by Poles on the outside.

I camped out on the banks of the Vistula River for many days and nights nursing my injuries, then followed train tracks that ran east, more or less. I wanted to move on, to get as far away from the ghetto as possible but it was proving impossible to cover much ground with the pain in my legs. One morning as I lay resting in a ditch near the edge of a field I overheard men's voices speaking French. What were they saying? Peering out from the high grass, I made out three or four workmen with picks and shovels coming down the road. I thought I'd heard something about "people from Belgium." I listened carefully now. One of the men was saying, "There are Belgian laborers in Minsk Mazowiecki." Belgian laborers! I thought immediately of my parents. But where was this place, and how could

I ever find it?

Creeping along at a tortoise pace, I continued to follow the railroad tracks, hoping they would lead me to the town with the Belgian workers. Though I stayed within the shelter of trees, I knew by listening where the tracks were because I could hear long lines of cars roaring by at all hours. One night I awoke in the darkness and slowly became aware of muffled noises not far from where I lay. At first, I didn't know what they were—animal cries? I listened harder, then I suddenly recognized the sounds of human misery—sobbing, moaning, wailing—coming from the direction of the tracks. Oh, God! What now? I thought. In a panic I dragged myself up and stumbled on, away from the tracks, away from the nightmarish noises.

Behind me I left, sidetracked and waiting in the dark, a line of closed and boarded up boxcars filled with human cargo bound for the gas chambers at Treblinka.

Early on the Warsaw Ghetto held 450,000 Jews. Thousands of them died every month—100,000 in two and a half years—mainly from disease and starvation (Jews were officially allowed rations of only 184 calories per day.) Then the Treblinka death camp opened on July 23, 1942 to receive by train 300,000 Jews from the Warsaw Ghetto. The wealthy with money for bribes, the formerly powerful with connections in the right places, even the privileged Jewish police were not spared. All would eventually die by gassing and their bodies be burned in Treblinka's ovens. Before the end of the war nearly a million people would be murdered there.

In April of 1943, the few remaining prisoners, determined to die fighting, staged the now-famous Warsaw Ghetto uprising. Inmates who had been smuggling in weapons since the previous December were able to prevent the Nazis from deporting a single prisoner to Treblinka. Frustrated, the Nazis decided to liquidate the ghetto entirely, and on the morning of April 19 troops with tanks and heavy artillery began the offensive. The resistants were armed and ready. By two o'clock that afternoon, not a German soldier remained alive in the ghetto.

A month later the Nazis took their revenge by burning the ghetto to the ground. Of all those who faced death by bullets, gassing, suicide or fire only a handful escaped to bear witness to these events.

Now terrified of trains, I left off following the rails and instead picked up the river again as it wove its way through groves of fragrant evergreens and past grassy sloping banks where I could sit to bathe my sore legs. Eventually I reached the outskirts of a town—a graceful town of parks, winding streets and lovely cottages. It was not Minsk Mazowiecki and I did not see laborers of any kind there, but I did see something terrible. As I would learn later, this was Otwock, a picturesque health resort located a few miles southeast of Warsaw.

Though it was very early, the day's heat was opressive as I threaded my way past the elevated train station and along the tree-lined streets. I came to a public well where I stopped to get a drink of water. To the townsfolk milling in the street in the searing morning sun I was invisible. Would there be a chance here to find something to eat? Following along some distance behind a group of men in a hurry to get someplace, I reached the perimeter of a wide public square. A large crowd was gathered and I stopped to see what was going on. Suddenly a shot rang out from across the square. Immediately I bolted in the opposite direction, but just at that moment the throng broke apart and overtook me and I found myself in the middle of a panicked mob. There was screaming and jostling, then more shots, and I felt myself being shoved and pushed on all sides. Trying not to stumble and fall under those stampeding feet, I clung to the shirttails of a huge man in front of me who was elbowing his way efficiently through the teeming mass.

When we tore free, I let go of my unwitting benefactor and ducked into a gateway. From there I could see the source of the shots: Soldiers standing on the hoods of military vehicles were firing again and again into the mass of terrified, writhing bodies. Those closest to the rifles were hemmed in from behind and fell like targets in a carnival game. In one voice a wail of anguish rose from the crowd as men, women and children were slaughtered like cattle.

I looked around desperately for the fastest way to get out of there. Just then a group of eight or ten children dashed past me and fled down a narrow passageway. They appeared to know where they were going so I ran behind, catching up with them as they headed for the trees along the outskirts of town. Together we continued running deeper into the woods until we were all exhausted and fell to the ground gasping.

Then one of the children barked some kind of orders and they all began to dig with their hands in the sandy soil. Guessing they were making trenches to hide in I began to dig too. The children gathered the ferny branches of acacia trees, then crawled into their holes and covered themselves over. I followed their example.

Darkness came and quiet descended, except for occasional whispers between the children. Once down in my foxhole, my cautious brain began spinning: This was the first time in all my roaming that I'd been part of any group. I had sorely lacked companionship but I'd survived so far by depending on only one soul—myself. Once, when Grandfather was telling me to be my own person and not to trust others, I asked him, "What about children, Grandfather, can't I trust them?" and he had answered, "Kids are young adults." Well, I would keep that in mind, but I felt no immediate threat from these children so I fell fast asleep.

When I awoke at sunrise I knew immediately something was up. The children had risen and were chattering excitedly and scurrying around, shaking the bushes and reaching up into the tall branches.

Someone had sneaked in during the night and put pieces of bread all over the bushes. Who could have done a thing like this? I couldn't imagine it was some generous person taking pity on us; we were surrounded by enemies. It had to be some kind of trap, a trick. I knew immediately that we had to get out of there.

The children were laughing and playing catch with the bread as they stuffed their mouths. I grabbed a piece too, but all my instincts cried "danger" and I immediately threw it down. Frantic, I gestured to the others, "Come on, let's get out of here!" but they looked at me as though I were crazy and kept eating the bread. I grasped the sleeve of a girl about my age and tried to pull her along with me but she drew back. I wanted to help them, to warn them, but what more could I do? The alarm was screaming in my head, "Get out! Get out!" I began running as fast as I could deeper into the forest.

I tell this story because I lived it. At the time, the experience reinforced my conviction that my survival depended on my traveling alone.

Were the children captured? Were they harmed? Who put the bread there? I have no answers to these questions. After the war, in a Jewish newspaper, I read about the slaughter of Jews in Otwock. Many people died, many also escaped according to the account, but the children were presumed lost; the only signs of them were the holes that were discovered in the thicket.

The killing spree I witnessed at Otwock was not an isolated event. At any moment, in any part of the occupied zone, the Nazis would round up Jews and simply exterminate them on the spot.

After leaving Otwock, I would pass close to the Polish town of Minsk Mazowiecki. I had no way of knowing it was so near and so I never had the chance to search for my parents there.

Instead, I continued my journey eastward.

CHAPTER 6

At the beginning of my long odyssey it had been fairly easy for me to identify the regions of Europe I passed through. The areas of the Ukraine that I crossed in 1943 and 1944, however, are a blur of farms, forests, villages, dialects and seasons. During all my travels, I had nothing with which to measure time or distance— no clock, no calendar, no map. Not until many years later was I partially able to piece together the whens and wheres of my journey.

As there was no structure in my life, there also was no consistency. I walked when I wanted to walk and stopped when I wanted to stop, usually to befriend a wild creature that came my way. In the middle of the night I might awaken at some suspicious noise and move on, then sleep the next day.

When human food was available, I ate whatever I could get. When there were no kitchens to raid or crops to forage, I managed on insects, such as grasshoppers and crickets, and their larva. I consumed nuts, particularly acorns and chestnuts, and all kinds of vegetation, tubers and seeds. I ate dandelions—yellow pincushion flowers, leaves and even roots, when necessary—chicory, wild gooseberries, juniper berries which tasted bad and made me drowsy and the tiny pear-shaped red berries which grew on prickly low bushes with silver leaves (sea buckthorn.) Catching fish became easier when I figured out that I could herd them into shallow water and then simply scoop them up in my hands. I also ate frogs and any kind of mammal that I didn't have to kill myself, always raw for I was afraid to use fire. Sometimes my meals worked out quite well, as whenever I came across watercress growing in a stream bed, or rose hips in a brambly hedge, or little curled fern heads coming up through wet, brown leaves.

But sometimes my experiments with unfamiliar menus led to cramps and vomiting. By observing what the wild creatures ate and by a process of trial and error, I learned what was safe and what was not. When pickings were paltry, mimicking the deer, I peeled bark with my knife from pine saplings and scraped off the smooth layer beneath. This I'd chew for a long time, spitting out the fibrous material after I had extracted what I could. Birches, too, were especially good because I could use the white outer bark I peeled off as an extra layer of insulation inside my leggings. Their thin new shoots and buds provided me with many meals.

Because I tended to travel along streams and rivers, I usually had fresh water nearby to drink, in winter there was also snow, in summer, rain and dew. I had no set routines, however—no particular time to eat, wash, steal, walk, rest or sleep. The only surety was that one day followed another, one season gave way to the next.

The Ukraine
Spring, 1943

I was now following a river southward in what had long ago become a doomed attempt to locate the village of Minsk Mazowiecki.

Walking along the edge of a forest, I wondered how much longer my feet would hold out before I found a resting place for the night. My shoes were pressing painfully against my toenails. I took them off and lifted one foot, then the other, to my mouth and bit off each nail. Poor feet. I rubbed the soles and massaged my toes, now curved over like claws from miles of walking in ill fitting shoes, but I couldn't stop until I found a sleeping place.

Up ahead a thin trail led into dense, dark woods. The path snaked around a bit, and I hoped it wouldn't circle back to my starting point. I decided to follow it and see where it would take me.

The trail eventually led to a wide clearing in the woods and, on the far side, a steep hill topped by an outcropping of rock. That high spot would make a good place to sleep, I thought—out of sight from below but with a lookout view all the way around. The hill was steeper and higher than I'd thought and the climb arduous; I was ready to collapse by the time I reached the top.

I shall never forget the sight that met me when I stepped onto that rocky summit. Rolling and tumbling on the ground in mock combat were three fuzzy, gray wolf pups! My heart skipped a beat and I stood perfectly still, not daring to breathe lest I frighten them away. Where was their mother? I lifted my eyes and there, on a ledge a short distance away, was an adult wolf, fast asleep. As I stood there, a fourth pup, darker gray, came bounding out of an opening under the ledge. This was a den—the rock I'd been climbing to was a wolf den!

Slowly I bent my knees, dropped to the ground and began backing down the hill on all fours. Being upwind, the adult wolf had not picked up my scent as I approached, and I did not want to cause alarm by being too close when it did. Suddenly the sleeping wolf raised its head and sniffed the air. Spotting me, it sprang to its feet and growled deeply. I held still in a crouch and instinctively averted my eyes. The wolf advanced toward me suspiciously, ears forward, tail straight back, as the three pups scrambled to the opening of the den and disappeared.

I tried to make myself look small, as I had learned to do when Ita had threatened me. The wolf approached, its head extended, sniffing furiously, then circled me cautiously. I could feel its warm breath under my collar as its nose searched for clues to what manner of beast had stumbled onto its den. I did not move a muscle, hardly even took a breath.

After an intense inspection, I passed some kind of test because the wolf at last withdrew and returned to the ledge. I sat up slowly, quite sure that it had not completely lost interest in me. Long minutes went by while I sat perfectly still and the wolf on the ledge rested with its chin on its front paws. Eventually a small black snout appeared at the opening of the den. The pup ducked inside again but quickly reemerged with another fuzzy sibling, then a third and fourth. Once outside, they all looked over toward me warily, but I stayed motionless as a stone.

Within a minute they resumed their mock combat. I looked on in delight, not quite believing my good fortune. From its perch on the ledge the adult wolf was watching through half closed eyes while the pups enjoyed their game of pouncing, rolling and chewing on each other, communicating all the while in high-pitched "eey—eey"s.

After a long while I tentatively called out a single "eey—eey." The pups ignored me.

Again, I whined "eey—eey."

One of the pups bounded toward me but stopped short. I remembered I had a hunk of cheese in my knapsack and slowly reached in, broke off a piece and tossed it to the nearest one. The little fellow eyed the morsel with curiosity, crept up and sniffed it, recognized it as edible and instantly gobbled it up. The other three pups came up to sniff the crumbs and I tossed out three more chunks which just as promptly disappeared before they retreated again.

Inch by inch, I began slowly to crawl over to them, stopping and starting, being careful not to upset the watchful adult nearby. Holding another lump of cheese I extended my arm toward them, but kept my fingers closed over the treat. They began to sniff and lick my fingers, then paw at my hand, then circle around to see if there were another way to get at the prize. After a minute I opened my hand and they lunged at the cheese, trying to shove each other out of the way and growling with puppy fierceness.

In a short space of time we became friends. I rubbed more cheese on my clothes and lay on my back while they climbed all over me trying to lick it off. The sentry ambled over to have a sniff, too, but quickly lost interest and returned to its perch.

To the pups, however, I was an object of intense interest and they poked their wet little noses into every fold and cranny, sniffing for messages about who I was and how I fit into their world. Those little whiskers in my neck tickled so much that I laughed out loud. Then they began to lick my knapsack which smelled of all the food I ever had transported in it. I studied them too: two males and two females. Their eyes had lost the baby blue color of very young animals but their coats were still soft and downy and they had short little legs and stocky bodies. The dark pup's ear had a nick in it and I would later name this little ruffian "Split Ear".

They quickly accepted being stroked and tickled and responded by licking and mouthing my hands and arms. When the pups took playful bites, I gently bit them back. In the magic of the moment my exhaustion evaporated and we all five began to chase each other, rolling, feinting and ambushing all over the hilltop.

When the ruckus got too animated, the baby-sitter on the ledge raised its head and looked at us, in much the same way that adults indulgently regard boisterous children. In that moment of paradise I forgot all about the pains in my body and the pains in my heart. Playing with those pups, I was a child again; there was no war or cruelty or death for me. No, I was something better: I was a wolf pup.

The sun was setting when the pups and I finally lay still in the grass, panting from our games. Not wanting to push my luck by moving in on the wolves too quickly, I decided to spend the night some distance from the den and come back the next day.

When I awoke the next morning, I immediately set off for the village to hunt for food and was lucky to find what I wanted in the first house I entered. Heading back with a full knapsack I began to plan how I would share some with the pups. I cut a slab of bacon into small pieces which I wrapped in leaves and stuffed in my knapsack then ate the rest on the spot. I was so excited about seeing the pups again that I galloped all the way up the hill, but when I reached the top, sweat running into my eyes, there were no pups in sight. Were they sleeping in their den under the rock ledge?

I turned and starting to head back to my home base when suddenly I spotted a large golden wolf stalking warily up the embankment. The body language—neck outstretched, hackles up—was unmistakable; I'd seen that menacing behavior in Ita. Instinctively, I threw myself on my back as I'd done with him. The wolf approached and began sniffing me from top to bottom. I hoped with all my heart that the animal would pick up the scent of the pups from yesterday and decide I was acceptable.

Instead it picked up the scent of a meal and began to chew on my knapsack. I quickly extracted the meat and the wolf made short work of it before resuming its inspection of me. While this was going on, all I could think to do was to whine "eey—eey" a few times like a wolf pup. Finally the wolf stepped back and looked at me with a puzzled expression. I "eey-eey"d again. At last it turned slowly and walked away. I was accepted!

Eventually I befriended the entire pack, six adults in all, plus the four pups. Within the next few days, they each subjected me to similar scrutiny, with the same result. I took my time getting to know them. At the beginning I slept some distance from the den, not wanting to crowd them lest they decide to move away. Each day I spent a little more time on the rocky plateau until one evening I spread my oilcloth right next to the opening to the den where the pups slept. From that time on, the wolves' hilltop home was my home too.

The chief of the pack was a big, rust-colored male with a dark face. He and the golden wolf, whom I called "Beauty," were the parents of the four pups. The "baby-sitter" that I'd met that first day was an old female with white whiskers who often bore the brunt of Beauty's aggression. Two other females, "The Twins," and a male, whom I dubbed Moonlight because of the white spots on his front paws—youngsters from last year's litter—also took turns as baby-sitter during a hunt or looked after the pups when they were around.

But often they were all gone except for the designated baby-sitter—usually the old female. As with all wolves, the business of this pack was hunting, which they carried out almost daily. Preparations for the hunt usually began with a ritual in which the adults assembled to nuzzle and gently nip or bump each other, wagging their tails and frisking around in the friendliest manner.

Soon one of them would begin to howl, sometimes while lying on its side, sometimes sitting or standing. Within seconds the others would wander over and join in, including the old baby-sitter and even the pups—ten puckered muzzles would point heavenward as the pack chorused their haunting refrain. Then Beauty and her mate and the three young adults would set off together while the old wolf resumed her place on the ledge overlooking the pups' "playground."

Seeing the strong family ties between members of the pack, I felt not only deep sadness for my own shattered family but also gratitude for the chance to be a member of theirs.

While the wolves were gone I would head off to the village to pilfer my dinner. This became a much more frequent event than it had been when I traveled alone because I was unable to set anything aside for consumption at a later date. Since our first encounter when I introduced them to my food, the pups began to look forward to these treats. There was no way I could hide extra provisions for tomorrow's meal; their favorite activity was exploring my knapsack. If I had anything edible their keen noses immediately discovered it, and they would pester me until I turned it over.

I had to be very careful with my knapsack around the puppies. It was my most precious possession and I never took it off. It always hung beneath my arm except when I lay down to sleep. Then without removing the strap I would twist it up to use as a pillow under my head. It was threadbare now and the strap had been broken and retied several times so that it hung higher than it had when it was new, but I clung to it like a prayer. Even when it was empty of anything edible the pups were attracted to its rich and varied odors, so I would have to open it up for them and show the inside saying "See? Nothing there. But just wait, your Maman's coming soon and she'll have a good dinner for you."

I enjoyed bringing back gifts from my pilfering forays, but when one of the puppies got hold of a whole piece of meat or bread from my knapsack he would take off with it at top speed with the others chasing along behind hoping for a share. Since I hated to see any of them go hungry I usually divided the prize into four portions before I showed it to them and made sure they all got their due. However, as a consequence of my friendship with these little "bottomless pits," I often went without a meal myself.

Then one day, as I watched the pups greet Beauty on her return from a hunt, an idea occurred to me. I had watched this ritual many times: When their mother appeared on the grassy plateau outside the den, the pups immediately ran to her and began licking and nipping at her muzzle and whimpering insistently. After a few moments Beauty's back arched and she regurgitated a mound of red meat chunks, as fresh looking as some of what I'd pilfered from kitchens. The pups devoured them on the spot. I had seen this behavior with the other adults produce the same result: dinner for the puppies and even the baby-sitter. Now I began to wonder if it would work for me.

The next day while returning from an unsuccessful jaunt in the village, I discovered, quite near the den, the remains of a freshly killed fawn. When I reached the plateau, the pack had just arrived too and it was apparent from their distended bellies that they had eaten well, and there would be plenty for the pups, too. I decided to try some of their meal. The adult wolves were engaged in their usual rounds of greetings, wagging their tails and nuzzling the pups who gathered around them whining imploringly. Within a few moments Beauty arched her back and brought up a mass of shredded deer meat. The four puppies fell on the pile and began to devour it greedily. I walked up to the group and reached my hand over their squirming bodies to take a piece.

Suddenly Beauty let out a snarl and leapt at me. Knocking me on my back, she stood over me stiff legged, her bared fangs just inches from my neck. I froze, not daring to breathe. But then she lifted her head slightly and her lips eased down to cover those fearsome teeth, though she still held her menacing position. I lay perfectly still for several long moments, then, when Beauty seemed to relax a bit more, tried a few meek puppy whimpers. Apparently she decided she had made her point because she turned from me and walked back to her youngsters.

Despite the discipline meted out to me then—and later—I was never truly afraid of any of the wolves. If I inadvertently violated their hierarchy, they might snarl or even snap their teeth, but I always felt the gestures were a warning, a way of showing who was boss, rather than a sign of true danger.

In fact, after this incident, I immediately decided to try again. I guessed that my mistake had been that I did not imitate the puppies exactly. When the pups had eaten their fill, I got on my hands and knees and crawled over to Beauty, uttering little whines and squeaks as they had done. Mustering all my courage, I pushed my nose between her lips. She turned her face away but didn't seem to be offended. I tried again, this time licking and nipping her muzzle as the pups did, and—success!—Beauty lowered her head and delicately dropped, right in front of me, a small pile of warm, shredded meat with a few bone shards for crunch. I was hungry enough that I didn't stop to think about what I was eating.

Later that evening the adult wolves left for short intervals, coming back with huge bellies, and meaty trophy bones for the puppies. The following afternoon I again passed the deer carcass. There was nothing left but the stomach and hide.

The pups made fast work of the bones the adults carried back for them. They were getting new teeth and chewed incessantly on everything they came across, including branches, rocks and—me, when they had the chance. In one week the lowest branches of all the surrounding bushes were stripped off and carried away, and the ground outside the den was strewn with the remains.

One day I returned from an outing to find all the pups arranged in the center of the clearing, spoke-fashion, noses pointing to the center. Right there beside them was Moonlight, the baby-sitter for the day. So deeply engrossed in some activity were they, that they didn't even look up when I arrived. But as soon as I approached to have a look, Moonlight suddenly jumped to his feet, grabbed the object of their attention and took off with it, the pups right behind. With dismay I recognized what it was: my boot!

I had left my spare boots hanging by their laces from a nearby tree, out of their reach. What I hadn't taken into account was that they had been growing and now could reach my formerly safe "closet." It was obvious from the many tatters of soggy, tooth-marked leather strewn on the ground that the boot was long past usefulness.

The second boot, which was lying at the opening of the

den, had fared better. I started over to pick it up, but when Moonlight saw me heading in that direction, he made a dive and a grab and took off with it at top speed, his ears streaming out behind. I headed him off and tackled him as he went flying by, knocking him on his back and landing on my belly with a thud. The boot hit the ground, closer to me than Moonlight and I made a lunge for it. Just as my fingers touched it, however, another set of teeth, little Split Ear's, snatched it from my almost-grasp and off it went in the opposite direction with the other puppies running interference. The boot was last seen disappearing into the den where it was, no doubt, demolished at the pups' leisure in a place where I did not intrude.

Too young to go hunting with the adults, the pups staged increasingly competent mock hunts on the grassy plateau, stalking and ambushing each other for hours on end. When a hapless mouse wandered into their midst, however, they had no idea what to do with him. All four sniffed him from a distance, not showing much enthusiasm for a closer encounter. When the mouse became confused and began to run toward the novice hunters, they backed away, afraid of the tiny creature. The mouse eventually found its way to safety without so much as a scratch to boast of from its encounter with four young wolves.

I remember sitting for hours with my back against a boulder, watching the puppies at play, while overhead two birds chatted, endlessly repeating a call that sounded oddly Russian:

"Teet-teet, tarabishkovitch?"

"Teet-teet, tarabishkova!"

When the pups tired of their games, one by one they trotted over to where I was, climbed on top of me and dozed off. In order to avoid disturbing them, I stayed perfectly still, but eventually my legs went numb under their weight. I readjusted carefully and soon I, too, fell fast asleep, blanketed by wolves.

Days became weeks and weeks became summer. Sunny days and cool nights wrapped me and my wolf family in such a cloak of peace that I rarely thought about moving on. By now I was being treated as a member of the pack and was greeted after each absence with wagging tails and exuberant muzzle-nuzzling. Whenever I injured myself, usually by playing too roughly with the pups, I'd go over to one of them and say, "Come on, my friend, lick me, cure me!"

I enjoyed the privileges of sleeping where they slept and eating what they ate, although on a more modest level. My low rank in the group was indicated by the fact that I was always the last to dine, even if I had provided the meal. After the incident with Beauty I was careful not to overstep my bounds, although I did make one other slip.

I wanted so much to become a wolf that I imitated everything they did. One day I made the mistake of relieving myself in the manner of the Chief and Beauty: by lifting my leg on a nearby rock. Immediately Beauty was over me, snarling a warning. Later I realized that only the dominant pair in the pack peed with a raised leg. The other females squatted and the males just stood foursquare and aimed downward. Because I was the lowest member, when I wet a particular spot, one or another wolf would invariably come over and make its mark on top of mine.

Still among the wolves, for perhaps the only time in my life, I did not feel like an outsider. One day I learned how accepted I really was. The entire pack was assembled on the plateau preparing to set out on a hunt. I planned to head into the village later myself but, feeling tired, I climbed up to the ledge over the den and lay down in the warm sunshine to rest a minute. Suddenly I was awakened by the yelps of a particularly rough mock battle among the puppies. One pup had suffered a nasty bite to his ear. Looking around for the baby-sitter I realized with a shock that the pack was gone; there was no adult wolf here—I was the baby-sitter!

I knew well the total devotion the whole pack showed to the puppies and understood what a statement of trust the adults had made by leaving them in my care. Their trust was well placed—I would have risked my life to protect them.

Throughout that magical autumn I got to know the pack well. Each animal was an individual, with a unique appearance, personality, and even voice. When I would hear howling in the distance, I could recognize each member by its tone of voice and style. I always howled along so I suppose I developed my own style too.

With the coming of winter I was well on the way to becoming a wolf. Although my body was less able to mutate than my mind, one day I took a good whiff of myself and recognized that musky wolf odor. It would have been easy to wash myself and my clothes in a stream, but I loved my wolf perfume and wanted to keep it.

The wolves also liked to perfume themselves. Any really stinky thing one of them happened to find would quickly draw the whole crowd. With obvious pleasure each would take a turn rolling and rubbing its neck and back on the smelly treasure on the ground. They were particularly fond of rotten fish and decomposed dead bird. Much as I loved them, I couldn't quite convince myself that I liked their taste in scents.

The days with my wolf family multiplied. I have no idea how many months I spent with them but I wanted it to last forever—it was far better than returning to the world of my own kind. Today, though most memories of my long journey are etched in tones of gray, the time spent with the wolves— like my days in the Ardennes—are drenched in color. Those were the most beautiful days I had ever experienced.

The territory surrounding the wolf den was crisscrossed with dozens of trails scored into the forest floor by the wolves and the game they hunted. Often I wandered along them, accompanied by one or more of the youngsters, who were beginning to show signs of growing independence. On this day Moonlight and Split Ear were tagging along, staying within howling range (they would come running when summoned by a howl) but pursuing their own interests. My mind wasn't on pups, however, but on wild raspberry bushes that grew all along the path. The best bushes were always just a little farther along. I was so engrossed in my berry picking that I didn't notice when my companions disappeared.

My mouth was stuffed with berries when out of nowhere I heard a scream. Instantly I dove into the brush beside the trail and hid, tense and alert, peering through the branches. Someone was moving close by—a man—a German soldier. He was dragging something along the path—no not something, someone—a young girl.

He hadn't seen me! I craned my neck to get a better view. He was coming along the path with her and heading in my direction. I put my head down and lay flat on the ground, holding my breath.

Where were they now? I could see nothing, but I could hear the girl screaming. I lifted my head and pulled the branches apart carefully, trying unsuccessfully to get a view of them. Then, as they came closer, they were framed in the opening.

The girl kept collapsing on the ground like a rag doll, trying to pull out of the soldier's grasp, but each time he would jerk her up, limp and flailing. As they approached I looked into her terrified face. She was so young, hardly more than a child.

They stopped just a few feet from my hiding place. I pressed myself flatter to the ground and watched, horrified, as he threw her down, knelt beside her and began to tear at her clothing. Pleading with him, she tried to cover her nakedness with pale thin arms, tears streaming down her cheeks. Still he continued berating her and ripping the dress from her huddled frame. Suddenly he raised his arm and struck her back-hand across the face. She let out a sharp cry and fell to the ground. The soldier immediately threw himself down on top of her and began pounding her with his body. She cried out again and again, and with each anguished cry I flinched too.

Then everything became deathly still. Moments passed. I lifted my head slightly. Had she fainted? The soldier stood up, as casually as if he were rising from a good meal. He walked around the girl's prostrate form and nudged her with the toe of his boot. She did not move. His pants were open and his sex was covered with blood. He drew his pistol from its holster, spat on her, then calmly shot her.

I must have jumped at the explosion, because suddenly he looked directly at the spot where I was hiding. I stopped breathing and lay perfectly still. He peered intently, then started walking deliberately toward me, buttoning his fly as he came. I rolled over on my back, slowly pulled my dagger from its scabbard on my belt and gripped it tightly against my leg. As filthy and bedraggled as I was, if he found me, perhaps he would take me for dead.

"Lie still! Don't move!"

I turned my head away and held my breath. My eyes were closed, my face composed to appear lifeless, but my mind was racing. How stupid to die now—and for what? For those damn raspberries! I had been so concerned about them that I had wandered too close to the edge of the woods. If I'd been watching the wolves and noticed their departure I'd have known there was trouble ahead. It was so clear—Mishke, Mishke, what a fool you've been!

The forest was so still I could hear the crunch of leaves under his boots as he drew near. There was a rustling in the brush close by.

Then—silence.

Without opening my eyes I knew—he had found me!

I lay perfectly still, but every one of my senses was hyper-alert, every muscle in my body taut as a coiled spring.

"Not me!"

I heard the rustle of fabric near my ear. I sensed that he had kneeled down and was bending over me. My lungs were bursting; I needed to take a breath.

"Not me!"

He was above me. I could feel him inhaling, exhaling against my cheek! My heart was pounding so hard I was afraid he could hear it. The decision was made...

"Now!"

The dagger struck him in the belly. I felt it go in all the way to the hilt. My eyes flew open and I saw everything in fine detail and slow motion: his face right over mine, his eyes wide with surprise, both hands clutching the dagger as it withdrew. When he opened his hands we both looked down: the knife had sliced his fingers deeply and blood was beginning to ooze from the clean, red cuts. Then his whole weight fell on me, pinning me to the ground.

No! I shoved with all my strength, twisted away and jumped up. He began to raise himself on his hands and knees, struggling to stand. My dagger struck him in the shoulder, in the neck—could it take out his eyes so he couldn't see me?—again and again the dagger rose and fell; it had a will and life of its own.

Everything in my vision was red, the soldier, the dagger, the air itself. Blood was everywhere, all over him, all over me. Still he did not fall, but instead raised his head. I looked right into his eyes and he into mine. Then he stretched out one hand to fend me off and with the other reached for his gun.

No! No! No!

That's for that girl over there.

That's for my mother and father.

That's for my Maman Rita.

For the starving people in the ghetto.

For the slaughtered of Otwock.

For Marek.

For me.

For the child I never was.

There! There! There!

At last he toppled over and lay still, face down in the dirt, and I collapsed next to him. I was gasping and trembling, but in a moment I realized that I was physically unhurt. Slowly, I wiped my dagger on his uniform and put it back in its scabbard, then mechanically as a robot, I removed the gold watch from his wrist and put it in my pocket. I replaced a shoe that had come off in the struggle, pulled myself to my feet and turned away.

For some time I had been zigzagging through the forest in a daze, not knowing where I was or where I was going. At last I stopped and slumped against a tree. I looked down: pink tears, colored with blood, were falling onto my bloody hands. The smell of blood was in my nose, the metallic taste, in my mouth. My clothes were sticky with blood; with trembling hands I felt my face and my hair—

wet too. I was shaking uncontrollably.

My head fell back against the tree. "Hold on. Hold on." Then through my tears I saw them—Split Ear and Moonlight. They scarcely recognized me, unfamiliar as I appeared now, and so they stood, heads cocked with curiosity, watching from a cautious distance. I leaned forward and tried to call to them but no words came. Then Moonlight suddenly caught on and bolted toward me, with Split Ear close behind. At that moment, the floodgates opened and wrenching sobs overtook me.

The pups jumped on top of me and began to lick me all over as I slumped limply, unable to respond, letting them clean my face and hands. How long did I stay like that? I have no idea. When at last I stopped trembling, I rose unsteadily to my feet and stumbled to a nearby stream, the pups beside me all the way.

I collapsed in the cool water and peeled off my bloody clothes. Using a chunk of bark as a brush I scoured and scrubbed the blood from my body. All the while in my head a voice kept repeating, "I'm alive. I'm alive."

But when I came out of the water and joined the pups, it all welled up inside me again, all the terror, all the horror. I lifted my face to the heavens and opened my mouth to scream, but seconds passed and nothing came. Finally, my throat unlocked and I heard a wailing sound, and it went on and on and on. The pups, too, began howling and so we howled together that afternoon, a chorus of sorrow.

CHAPTER 7

The Ukraine
Autumn, 1943

SUMMER WAS SLIPPING AWAY AGAIN. The night before, for the first time since last spring, I had slept with my winter jacket on. That morning the wolves had returned at dawn and were now stretched out on their sides in the thin, watery sunlight, sleeping off a big meal. All of them, the adults and the pups—though you could hardly call them pups anymore—had returned from their long hunt with greatly distended bellies and immediately flopped down where they lay. I knew they could sleep away the entire day before setting out at dusk to hunt again.

I watched them dozing peacefully, their ears automatically twitching away flies, their sides rising and falling with their rhythmic breathing. I lay among them, not peacefully, but beset by demons. They could go on like that for hours, but I was getting restless. What could I do other than sleep myself?—and I wasn't tired. When the wolves were gone on a hunt or sleeping like that, I had plenty of time on my hands to think about all the things I didn't understand.

I thought about the past, how my family had been hunted just like the wolves of the forest. Like them, my family was always on the move and each time we got to a new place we had a new name. My parents were afraid to tell me our real surname because it would identify us as Jews. I remembered my mother was called Gerusha, my father Robert, or sometimes Reuven in Hebrew, but our last name?—I think I never knew. That fact, I later realized, probably saved my life. As a "nobody," I was not named on any list, as were those who were rounded up and sent to the camps and the ovens.

I thought about all the food from all the homes I'd raided while the occupants were in church and about the people I'd seen in the ghetto, starving to death. I couldn't make sense out of it: Why were some people praying while others were dying? Instead of kneeling in church, why weren't all those pious people marching outside the gates of the ghetto, their voices and their fists raised in outrage, demanding that the people inside be set free? Why didn't they batter down the walls and take those pitiful souls into their homes and offer them bread, as any decent person would do for a starving dog?

Was it possible the people outside didn't know what was going on in the ghetto? How could that be? Outside the ghetto, death announced itself by the smell that went right over the wall; I had smelled it on the outside myself. I felt contempt for all those who turned their backs on the ghetto.

And why did those inside the wall seem so defeated? Why didn't they claw their way up the walls as I had done—push each other up and over? It seemed to me there were so many Jews and so few soldiers; if all the Jews rose up at once the soldiers couldn't stop them all, could they? Better to be gunned down fighting for freedom than starve to death in a filthy cage. How could those people let themselves be starved and slaughtered like that?

My thoughts troubled me greatly because I never came up with answers. Then I began to wonder why I stayed with the wolves instead of moving on. Why wasn't I making some attempt to find my parents? But when the pack finally awoke, I found such sweetness in their company that I forgot all about my mission.

The pups, now almost full-grown, had spent the summer honing their hunting skills on small rodents and rabbits and now had graduated to tagging along when the adults went off on a foray, leaving me alone. Of all of them, Moonlight was my favorite. Now an adult, he was turning into a trouble maker. He never passed up an opportunity to harass his siblings with a bite or a bump. When he was chewing on a bone or a stick, woe to the animal who tried to take it away, though he was not above snatching another's prize whenever he got the chance.

One afternoon as I was watching him playing roughly with one of the younger pups, I said to myself, "That fellow is getting too big for his boots." No sooner had the thought occurred to me than the Chief arrived on the plateau with a large, dirt-encrusted bone he'd apparently unearthed from a cache nearby. The big wolf settled himself in the sunlight with the bone between his front paws, closed his eyes and began gnawing contentedly.

Moonlight ceased chewing on his sister's flank and looked over at his father. I stared in horror at what happened next: Moonlight lowered his body into a crouch and began stalking the Chief, as I'd seen him do many times with the puppies. Slowly he crept across the plateau, inch by inch, readying himself for an ambush.

The big wolf had his back to the action so he was taken completely by surprise when Moonlight dove for the bone.

The Chief let out an outraged snarl and rose like a shot, every hair standing on end. He looked twice his normal size! With fangs bared he fell upon Moonlight, seized him by the neck and flung him to the ground. Instead of submitting, Moonlight immediately twisted out of his grip, got to his feet and held his turf. The Chief lunged again, caught Moonlight by the shoulder and the two animals, growling savagely, fell to the ground, a writhing mass of snapping teeth and flailing limbs. Suddenly Moonlight broke away and ran down the hill, ears laid back, tail so far between his legs it disappeared, with the Chief in hot pursuit. Several times as they ran the old wolf got Moonlight by the rump and pulled him down, but each time Moonlight's youthful agility enabled him to twist away and evade the snapping teeth. At last, Moonlight managed to put enough distance between himself and his father so that the older wolf gave up the chase and returned to the plateau to nurse his affronted pride and guard his bone.

Moonlight didn't return to the pack that day or the next. I missed him and kept wondering whether he had been badly injured in the battle. Then several days later when I was on a trail some distance from the den, I heard a familiar howl and followed the call until I located him standing at the crest of a hill. I immediately headed up the slope to greet him, breathing a sigh of relief that he was all right.

He wagged his tail as I approached but didn't come forward to meet me. When I got closer it became obvious that he was considerably worse off for his encounter with the Chief. There were bite marks, mostly superficial, all over his body and he looked thin and miserable. I stopped a little distance from him and reached into my knapsack.

"Come, my sweetness, I have a little meat for you. Come on, you look hungry—take a piece."

As he came up to get the meat I'd thrown, I decided right on the spot to follow my rebel friend from then on, to go where he went and share whatever I had with him.

It may have been a couple of weeks, or perhaps a month that I could count on Moonlight to be nearby or at least to seek out my company every so often. Then at some point, for some reason, he disappeared, and I was alone.

After he left I missed him, but I understood finally that it was time for me to move on. Earlier, during the long hours I spent watching the pack fast asleep, I had thought long and hard about Maman and Papa. Despite the passage of time, my need for them was as great as ever. In the company of my wolves I was so happy the yearning was assuaged for a while. But now, all by myself, I felt guilty about the time I'd spent following the pack instead of pursuing my quest.

With Moonlight's disappearance, the last excuse for staying had vanished too. I peered into the tiny compass now as if it were a crystal ball, studying the wavering needle and the letters marking north, south, east and west. I could still picture Grandfather's maps in my head. Home was west but I didn't want to cross back through Poland and into Germany. Perhaps if I went south I might come to a place where there was no war and it would be easier to find something to eat.

Winter, 1943

The ground I lay on was hard and cold, and my belly ached with hunger. I'd had nothing to eat for two days, and I was shivering so hard I couldn't fall asleep. I sat up and ran a hand over my scabs—injuries sustained in sliding down a tree. The day before I had climbed a huge beech and lain cradled in the junction of two branches for part of the night. As I was climbing down, I fell and scraped my wrists badly. Now I took out my knife and carefully sliced off bits of dried scabs. To have something to swallow I chewed on the crumbs of dried blood. (To this day I still nibble on any little scab that comes off; I can't bring myself to brush it away.)

The sky was turning gray. Day was coming. I picked up my oilcloth and adjusted my knapsack, pulled the collar of my jacket tighter around my neck and walked on along a dirt road across the open prairie. With no trees for cover, I felt constantly uneasy, though I rarely encountered any sign of people. For miles and miles there was nothing but long, bleak vistas of withered grasslands stretching to the horizon—no farmhouses, no plowed fields to scrabble for a bit of sustenance, no barns with grain or fodder. I was too weak to go on but afraid if I sat down I might not get up again. Somehow I kept walking until dusk, finding nothing to eat along the way.

By now I was so desperate with hunger that when I spotted in the distance, almost hidden in a stand of saplings, the stooped form of an old woman gathering branches and twigs, I deliberately walked into her line of vision. As soon as she saw me she stood up, though her back was still bent, and squinted at me with curiosity. She had a face as brown and shriveled as a year-old apple with a thousand wrinkles in which were set startlingly pale gray eyes. Wisps of fine white hair escaped from the black scarf around her head. If she was surprised to see me she didn't show it.

Although I was starving and exhausted, I mustered all my strength and lifted the sling from her bent back and began helping her gather sticks. The sling, which was fashioned from a tattered shawl, was soon bulging. She then led me to a tiny log cabin with a thatched roof. Still we had not said a word.

As we finished stacking the wood beside the door, she turned and addressed me. Russian! I recognized it immediately. That was what my mother spoke when she didn't want me to know what she was saying. I shrugged that I didn't understand and made my begging-for-food gestures. She nodded and gestured for me to follow her into the house, but I stood firmly planted outside the door. I knew it would be warmer inside but my deep distrust prevented me from sharing such close quarters with a possible enemy. Once again, I gestured that I wanted food. The old woman turned and closed the door but returned shortly holding a bowl of warm milk and a piece of brown bread. She stood watching silently as I wolfed it down. When I'd devoured the last crumb and licked the milk bowl clean, she again gestured for me to come inside, but I shook my head "No."

Though I couldn't bring myself to enter her hut, that night, for warmth, I did sleep with my back against its log wall. When I awoke the next morning, I found another slab of bread and a bowl of milk on the ground in front of her door, set out for me as for a pet dog.

It was a bleak, gray morning but I'd had a piece of good luck in an unguarded kitchen, so my spirits were up. The village I had just left looked like all the villages I'd passed through lately, with its charred and abandoned houses, scarred, rutted roads and sad-eyed people. Trees once had lined both sides of the street but they long ago had been cut down for firewood, leaving ugly stumps sticking out of the frozen ground. Many of the kitchens I broke into had nothing whatever in the larder for me to steal. As elsewhere, people of this village had a roof over their heads but starvation at the door, as real a danger for them as for me. Still, poor as they were, these villages were my best chance to find something to eat, for there were no crops in the field at this time of year.

I remembered the pretty towns I had seen in Belgium long ago when my journey began; these I was seeing now were nothing like them. The war had ground away comfort, order and community, leaving only the barest subsistence. The landscape around the villages, too, was dismal and ravaged. Abandoned shanties with no windows and dirt floors stood forlornly in bare fields. When the weather was bitter I would sometimes seek shelter in one of these, but being inside any dwelling made me feel trapped and I would only do it out of dire necessity.

Today, people sometimes ask me how I kept walking day after day, month after month, year after year. The answer seems simple enough now, though at the time it was not something I knew consciously: What else could I do? Every country I passed through was occupied by the Nazis. Famine was everywhere and no place was safe.

All the villages I encountered were alike in their misery. I remember them now, not by name, but only for events that occurred in them.

As I walked along a path on the outskirts of one village I came upon an unexpected sight. Shambling toward me on the dirt road I spied an old man and beside him an animal, all skin and bones, that appeared to be a gray wolf. I stepped to the side of the road and waited as they approached.

Just then a young man strode briskly past me and stopped next to the old fellow, and the two began to chat in Russian. The wolf—it was a wolf—lay down listlessly on his side next to the man, staring blankly into the road. I moved closer to get a better look. The animal was wearing a crude leather harness with a metal chain attached to the man's waist. Something about the way the wolf held his head disturbed me, then I realized that his eyes were clouded over. He was blind.

As the two men continued their conversation the wolf began to chew on a patch of raw skin on his front paw. My heart went out to the poor creature. I reached into my knapsack and pulled out the piece of pork rind I had just stolen and held it behind my back, waiting. When the men weren't looking, I tossed it on the ground between the wolf's front paws.

Instead of gobbling it up as I expected, the wolf got to his feet, growled and backed away, his ears flat against his head. At this, the two men turned and looked in my direction. I smiled sweetly at them and they smiled back, then resumed their conversation. I sauntered over, picked up the rind and again offered it to the wolf. To my dismay, the animal again growled at me and refused to take it. I returned the rind to my knapsack and walked away.

As I continued trekking along the road, I was deeply troubled by the blind wolf's behavior. Why had he rejected me? I still wore the same clothes with the scent of Moonlight and the others; I smelled like a wolf, and yet this animal didn't recognize me as one of his own kind. I wanted so much to feed him, to be his friend. Why didn't he accept me as all the other wolves had?

I puzzled and thought, then suddenly the answer came to me. Of course it growled! Of course it pulled away from me! I had remembered how the baby-sitter wolf had behaved the same way whenever she crossed paths with Beauty, the top female. Beauty would often harass other pack members by nipping and pawing at them, particularly the old baby-sitter, who was clearly the weakest. When Beauty began to intimidate her she would cringe and back away. The blind wolf had done the same. What I had interpreted as a rejection was probably a sign that the blind wolf had taken me for a fellow wolf, the stronger one, in fact. It, being the weaker, had shied away. With this realization, I congratulated myself, "I am a wolf! I am a wolf!"

In another village I almost was blown to smithereens in an artillery attack as I was attempting to snitch a meal. It was broad daylight and I was hiding behind a hedge along a wall, waiting for a chance to break into a kitchen. When the first shells hit, unleashing a ball of fire and an ear-shattering boom, people in the street scattered in all directions, running into houses or taking shelter in doorways.

The deafening explosions came, one after another, seemingly from all sides, and billows of black smoke and sheets of orange flame rose above the rooftops. Folding my arms over my head I sank to the ground and shrank against the wall. With each concussion I squeezed my eyes shut and flinched, expecting to be blown away at any moment. Each breath I drew seared my throat as acrid waves of smoke rolled over my head. Above a row of houses being consumed in a wall of flames, the air shimmered with waves of intense heat. The roar of fire and the shattering of glass filled my ears.

Suddenly I became aware of something pressing against my leg. A little white dog crouched between my feet, looking up at me with eyes bulging with fear. I picked up the animal, hugged its quivering body to my chest and repeated, "It'll be all right, it'll be all right. Don't worry, it'll be all right."

An enormous explosion flung us backward against the wall and the ground itself shook with the impact. Two sitting ducks out there in the open, both the little dog and I were now trembling with wild panic. A section of the wall nearby crumbled and fell. I had to do something. I had to find shelter. Without thinking of the possible consequences, I pulled myself up off the ground and ran out into the street toward the nearest house, clutching the dog under my arm. With all my might I beat my fist against the front door. I could hear a woman's hysterical voice inside, but no one answered my knocks. I kicked at the door, please, please, open up, please take us in! The door did not move.

Long whistles preceded each new explosion. Terrified, I rushed to the next house and the next, but still no door opened for us. More explosions! and more! I collapsed and sobbed against the last unyielding door—oh, please open up, please give us shelter.

Then something remarkable happened—I stopped crying. Suddenly I found myself leaving the doorway where I was and going back in my mind to the farm and the time when the bombers had roared over Grandfather's head. What had he said when Marthe and I started to run for shelter? "They can get me here. If I'm going to die, I'll do it here, out in the open."

Oblivious to the danger all around me, I slowly rose and made my way back to the wall, where I crouched down, no longer trembling, the dog still clasped in my arms. As I recall that time, it seems to me the dog stopped trembling too.

When the bombing ended, a pall of thick, black smoke hung over everything and I could hear in the distance the crackling roar of a huge fire. One by one, people began cautiously emerging from their shelters, sobbing and calling the names of their loved ones. I left my hiding place and ventured out into the road. Hoping my little friend would be able to find his owner, I fled from the scene of chaos, leaving behind me a village engulfed in flames. In the confusion I think I managed to snitch something to eat.

What happened at the moment that vision of Grandfather appeared to me? I don't know; I can't explain it. I tell the story as I experienced it.

Whenever I entered any village I brought along a heightened sense of danger. In one, I remember seeing walls pockmarked with bullet holes and spattered with blood, the ground beneath littered with bits of brain and skull from someone's shattered head. Such a sight was a warning to be careful, but otherwise I was numb to it. In fact, once I picked a shawl off a dead body which I wore until the smell of death that clung to it finally persuaded me to endure the cold instead.

But in another village I almost became a smear of blood myself. I had gone into an empty barn next to the last house on the road looking, as usual, for anything at all to eat. As I crept across the wooden floor, I stubbed my toe on a raised board. When I bent down to examine it, I discovered trap door that concealed a crude ladder descending to a room below. Could someone have hidden food down there? Sacks of dried beans or crocks of sauerkraut? Exploring the dark, musty cellar by the narrow shafts of light that came down through the planks, I found only curtains of cobwebs and dust-laden, broken farm equipment—nothing to eat. As I was about to climb the ladder, I heard frantic cries some distance away—and other voices shouting in German. I crept to the farthest corner of the cellar and crouched under an overturned wheelbarrow, listening intently. A blast of gunfire made me jerk, then came round after round of shots that cut the waves of terrified voices sharply in mid-cry. This went on intermittently for an hour or more, followed by the grinding of motors starting up, the hum of vehicles driving away and then—utter silence.

I waited in the darkness for many hours listening intently but hearing no voices, no footsteps, nothing. The sun was setting when I crept out of my hiding place and breathed in the evening air. The village was deathly quiet; no lights shone in the windows, no smoke rose from the chimneys. I walked slowly, cautiously down the deserted main street. On either side of the road all the front doors gaped wide. Pouring through them and out into the street were all manner of household goods—chairs and tables, dishes, pots, lanterns, clothing and toys. At the end of the street lay a rubble of smoldering ashes where a building once stood. I turned a corner and came to a little open square. Spread out on a still wet lake of blood, lay the staring corpses of the former residents of this ordinary hamlet, men and women, young and old, twisted in unimaginable, grotesque positions, their bodies riddled with bullet holes; and among them, sometimes nearly concealed but not protected by an adult's body, lay the rag doll corpses of little children.

I had witnessed an episode in the creation of Hitler's New Order, a wave of massacres in which Germans slaughtered entire villages in an attempt to clean out the "undesirable" elements.

Winter, 1944

I was not the same little girl who started off into the woods to find her parents. At the beginning of my journey I had been transported by the beauty I saw all around me—the great blue dome of the sky, the rolling rivers, the tranquil forests, the myriad and wondrous creatures of the earth. I had felt triumph at the clever way I was able to fend for myself in this magical kingdom, and that triumph had been almost intoxicating.

Things were different now, times had changed. When the will to survive must be exercised every second of every day, when the spirit is shocked and tested at every turn, when even sleep does not give a moment's respite, the supreme effort to merely keep alive crowds out any space for joy. Now there was no triumph. I was not at the mountain top, I was clinging precariously to the wall of the abyss.

But no matter what happened, no matter what trials I faced, I believed I would never let go. My will to survive was like a core of magma at the center of my being. Like lava it flowed into my every impulse, every decision, burning away sweetness and turning my heart to stone. I could endure; there was no doubt about that. I had seen too much, I knew too much. I had looked into the eyes of the demon, peered into the void and seen the countenance of hatred, and I was hard enough and ready for it all. I had thought I would never see anything to surpass the evil I'd witnessed in the Warsaw ghetto. But I was wrong.

Early one morning as I was trekking along a hill top toward the white onion dome of a distant church just visible above the tree tops, I heard the hum of a motor growing louder as it approached. I looked out between the branches at a wide, tire-rutted road traversing the open land below. A large truck turned off the road and came to a halt in the middle of a field.

Immediately, two German soldiers jumped out of the cab, ran around to the back of the truck and flung open the doors. Two more soldiers leapt from the back, and these were followed by a tattered parade of young boys and girls. As they emerged the children stood meekly huddled together beside the truck, passive, like small zombies. Some of them were holding hands and, among all the dark little heads, one small blond girl at the edge of the group was hugging a rag doll to her chest. The soldiers ceremoniously herded the children across the field and up alongside a long pit that I hadn't noticed before. The men went up and down the line, adjusting the children by their shoulders so that they stood at the edge of the ditch. Nobody cried, nobody struggled. As if playing a game, the men paced off a distance between themselves and the children and turned. The order was given: Ready! Fire! Ready! Fire! As the bullets rained down on them the little blond girl clutched her dolly and stood silently. One by one, the children toppled into the ditch and, at last, she too fell and all that was left was the echo of gunfire ringing in my ears. The whole business took but a few minutes. I don't know what happened after that because I turned and bolted into the woods where I bent over and threw up repeatedly. Curiously, I did not cry at the time.

The woodland path was icy, and I had to tread carefully, clutching at overhanging branches for balance. Still the sun was feeling warmer on my head that day. Perhaps spring would arrive at last.

The memory of those murdered children haunted me unceasingly. I replayed the scene over and over in my head and still could hear the crack of the bullets that mowed them down. Some of them were so little. Were they smaller than I?

Suddenly it was very important for me to know my own size. I pressed my back against a straight sapling beside the trail. Raising my knife, I cut a slash in the tree just at the top of my head. I turned around and, starting from the bottom of the tree, placed my hands one above the other, counting each hand until I reached the mark. "I'm 10 hands high. That's my size. Just a little bigger," I thought, "than the blond girl with the doll."

There are times even now when a terrible sadness and hatred come over me. After all these years I cannot wake up from this nightmare. I will carry it with me to my grave.

I have always loved crows. When I was on my own their raspy caws often meant the possibility of something to eat, from corn ripening in a field to carrion. Whenever I heard their cranky arguing I'd think of wolves, for the crows would always be the first opportunists to arrive at a kill, hopping around cautiously, watching for a chance to grab a morsel even before the wolves finished eating.

One day when I was following a flock of noisy crows I was led not to corn or carrion, but to a meal nonetheless. As I crossed a field of high grass I saw a curl of smoke snaking its way heavenward above the trees. Smoke meant burning, and that meant people. Cautiously I approached to have a look.

The smoke, I soon discovered, emanated from the chimney of a large log cabin. Two women and a man were sitting on a stump in the front yard, elbows on knees, laughing in a friendly, relaxed way and puffing on cigarettes. The man wore a uniform—not German. Behind the cabin a couple of sheds leaned precariously, and nearby a horse was tethered to a tree.

The idea that I might be able to pilfer some real food made me linger longer probably than was prudent. I spent several days in the woods surrounding this camp, often hiding nearby in a tree where I could observe what was going on. At night I heard singing inside the cabin, beautiful Russian ballads, and even laughter. I had never encountered anything like this before. One day I must have crept too close because suddenly I felt myself being pulled up into the air by my jacket collar, like a cat by the scruff of the neck. I fought like a tiger, kicking as hard as I could, but the powerfully built man who held me kept me at arm's length. I soon realized that I would not be able to break away, and went limp.

When I had quieted down, he led me through the yard

and into the cabin. We entered a large room and the man pushed me forward toward the center where a group of people was gathered around a table, talking animatedly. Everyone turned to stare as I approached.

Then a uniformed man rose from middle of the group and stepped from behind the table to greet me. What struck me immediately was his face—virile, with intelligence and directness written all over it. When he spoke to me I was surprised again—this time by the gentleness of his manner, though I didn't understand a word he said. When I didn't respond to his questions, he said something to the people around him and they all stood up and filed out the door. As they were leaving, I studied this man. He had thick black hair and a beard, and his uniform was unfamiliar to me. When he turned his attention back to me his dark eyes held mine firmly. He tried asking my name by pointing to me and raising his eyebrows in a question, but I would not speak. Then he pointed to himself and said "Misha," obviously his name, so I nodded that I understood. His face broke into a smile and he reached out his hand and patted my head.

At this, something in me wanted to melt. The last person who had bestowed that gesture of affection on me was Grandfather—how many seasons ago? With both hands this "Misha" gently eased me down on a chair next to the table and called to a woman standing by the door— "Malka!" The woman hurried over and Misha laid his arm casually over her shoulder and they began talking. I watched them together. Misha, tall, broad shouldered, with deep creases etched in his tanned cheeks and squint lines around his eyes. This was a man who had spent much of his life outdoors. The woman's eyes clung to his face adoringly. He smiled at her, flashing a mouthful of even teeth, very white.

I looked around the large, sparsely furnished room. At one end stood a massive wood stove, its open doors revealing a mound of glowing embers. It had been so long since I had enjoyed the warmth of a fire, and the heat seeping into my body was so comforting I actually began to relax until I noticed, in another corner, twenty or more rifles propped against the wall.

Who were these people? Fighters of some kind. They weren't Germans so they might be the opposition. I recoiled at the idea that they might be killers like the guerrillas I had encountered in Poland. It wasn't a moral issue for me. I just didn't want to risk my life with them—didn't want any part of their violence. All I wanted was to live to be reunited with my parents.

The woman led me by the hand to a chair closer to the fire where I'd be warm. Then she left the house and returned a moment later with a covered pot which she set on top of the stove. In a few minutes I smelled the incredible fragrance of real cooked food. My mouth began to water; I could hardly wait. How long had it been since I'd had anything like that? When Malka handed me a steaming bowl of cabbage and potato stew, I tried to eat slowly, to make it last, but couldn't keep from gulping it down. She smiled watching me and gave me a second helping as soon as my bowl was empty.

Malka was young and darkly pretty and she had a soft voice that made me feel comfortable in her company. Later that day she introduced me to several children who were part of the camp, and that night she showed me where I was to sleep—in a space off the main room, on the floor with the other children. I had never met people like this before and I was intensely curious about them. I began to relax just a little.

On my second or third day there, as I was petting the brown horse tethered behind the cabin, Malka came up to me, took me by the hand and led me into the cabin. Misha, who had been in the yard, left the group he was with and followed us in. On his head he wore a hat made of dark brown fur. It fascinated me, or rather, he fascinated me because he looked so strong and dashing in it. I must have been staring at him when, as he took it off and tossed it on the table, he caught my look and smiled at me. What a beautiful smile! I felt myself blush.

It soon became clear why Malka had brought me in. She explained something to Misha, looking over at me as she talked, then he got up from his usual chair behind the table and faced me squarely. He pointed at me then began going through a pantomime, rubbing his chest, his legs, his armpits, then pointing at me. I didn't understand what he was getting at until he pretended to take something in his hand and rub it vigorously all over himself. Soap! A bath! Me? I blushed again.

I shook my head, "No, I didn't need a bath." I wasn't about to get undressed with all those people around. Misha must have sensed the reason for my discomfort because he and Malka led me into the next room where he took down a big wooden tub from the wall. They began filling it with pots of hot water from the stove in the main room. When the tub was full Malka brought clean clothes, a shirt, sweater, trousers and underpants, neatly folded, which she laid out on a chair next to the tub, along with a stiff brush, a bar of gray soap and a folded length of rough cloth for a towel.

I watched all the preparations sullenly but didn't budge. Misha started to leave the room and looked back over his shoulder. I still didn't budge. Then he beckoned to Malka to leave with him, and held up his finger to tell me to wait a minute. I heard him dragging something, which he held up in the door opening to show me—his chair. Then he placed the chair just outside the door and closed it almost all the way. I went over and peeked out to see what was going on. There was Misha, sitting on the chair with his back to the door, his arms folded tightly across his chest, as if to show me that no one would invade my privacy.

I shut the door all the way. Feeling more secure, I went over to the tub, quickly stripped off all my layers of clothing, grabbed the soap and the brush and stepped into the warm water. Though this was my first real bath since I had left the DeWaels', I didn't linger to enjoy it. I ducked my head and washed my hair, picking out the twigs and burrs, and scrubbed my body as fast as I could. In some places the dirt was so encrusted that I had to scrape it off and my skin began to bleed.

I climbed out of the water—leaving months of grime and debris floating on the surface—and hastily dried myself. On a table in the corner I found bandages, rolls of torn sheeting, that I wrapped around my oozing sores. Looking down at my naked body was an unfamiliar experi-

Looking down at my naked body was an unfamiliar experience and I was surprised at what I saw: the slightest hint of breasts developing where before had been all sinew and bone. It was interesting to find them there but the prospect of becoming a woman didn't particularly please me. Since men were physically stronger than women I preferred to see myself as a tom-boy.

When I opened the door to the main room I was startled at the reaction my appearance elicited: Misha and Malka burst out laughing. I had put on the clean clothes they'd given me well enough, but sticking out beneath them, right over my clean body, were my old filthy rags. Not wanting to give up their precious wolf smell, I had put them back on.

Misha slapped his thigh and roared with laughter and Malka doubled over, shaking so hard I thought she'd fall on the floor. It was contagious; suddenly I was laughing along with them. When was the last time I'd laughed with people? Not for years, not since Grandfather. I couldn't stop myself from liking them. Against my will I longed to take down the wall that encircled my heart and trust them. I'd never expected them to be kind and decent to me, but they were.

For the first time in years I wanted to talk to somebody, to confide in Misha as Marek had confided in me, to say "Listen! Listen to what happened to me." But he and his friends spoke Russian and I spoke French, and anyway I'd survived so many dangers by keeping my mouth shut, what point would there have been in taking risks now?

My days with these Russian partisans were more peaceful than any I had spent since I left the wolves. I had a warm place to sleep, hot meals and friendly company.

It would have been easy to slip out of there unnoticed. Unlike the camp of the Polish partisans, here no one guarded me, making sure I didn't try to get away. But I didn't slip out; on the contrary, I wanted to stay—partly out of curiosity, partly because I was exhausted. Since leaving the wolves, I had been traveling under the most arduous conditions. I sorely needed a rest and welcomed the opportunity to build up my strength.

The period that I spent with Misha's entourage was so different from my time with the Poles. Although they were as heavily armed as the Polish partisans, during the time I was with them they never exposed me to any violence.

Another difference I noticed: They seemed so much better off than the other group: They had a roof over their heads and warm clothes. They weren't grim and fearful; in fact, they laughed a lot, shouted and sang aloud whenever they pleased. Often several of them would jump into a rusty pick-up truck and drive to the village in broad daylight, as if the war didn't exist. Once, I even went with them.

And they were friendly. Even the man who had captured me, whose name I learned was Petia, turned out to be all right. In fact, the first night I was there, he shyly offered me a sip from his bottle. I recognized the same firewater I'd seen the Polish partisans drinking and this time I knew to pass.

Misha had a habit of whittling on a stick when he was thinking and I would sit nearby and just watch him dreamily. The knife he used was different from any I'd seen before. Its sturdy handle, curved inward for a good grip, held a blade that was black, not silver-colored, on both sides. Once when he caught me peering at the knife from where I sat, he offered to let me hold it. I examined it closely, turning it over admiringly in my hand, testing the grip and trying the edge on a twig. He watched me respectfully for several minutes—it must have been obvious that I knew how to handle a knife—then took it back and continued nicking away at his stick. I was flattered that he had let me handle it.

Though I was feeling stronger and more relaxed after my several weeks with this troop, it was not my plan to stick around forever. That was just as well, because one day I began to notice preparations underway, people packing up the contents of the cabin and stacking piles of goods and trunks by the door. Were they going on some sort of raid? I wondered. Everything in the house, including the weapons, was readied. The next morning it was all loaded into the wagons. I stood outside the door watching one group after another head down the road away from the cabin, and I wondered whether Misha would be going too. Only the pick-up remained in the yard. Finally he came out of the cabin wearing his fur hat and a coat over his uniform. He walked over to me, took me gently by the arm and motioned for me to get into the pick-up.

I shook my head "No." He released my arm and raised his eyebrows in surprise. Smiling, he beckoned with his hand and pointed down the road, but again I shook my head. Something told me not to do it. It was time for me to go it alone again. With sadness, I pointed to myself and then to the opposite direction, the direction I was going to take. Finally, I held up my hand to say good-bye.

Misha looked at me a long moment, then he put up a finger to tell me to wait and walked back into the cabin. In a minute he emerged carrying a large box that he set into the back of the truck and began rummaging in it while I waited and watched his broad back. At last he turned and squatted in front of me. Solemnly he presented to me three gifts: a fur hat just like the one he wore, a knife like his, with a black blade, and a loaf of bread. I looked down at the objects, then up at him and my eyes filled with tears. What could I possibly give him to express the gratitude I couldn't speak?

I fished in my pocket and drew out the gold watch I'd taken from the soldier I'd killed. My hand trembled slightly when I offered it to him. He looked hard into my eyes a moment before taking it, put it carefully in his pocket and ran his hand gently over my head, as if in a blessing. Then he climbed into the cab of the truck and drove off.

I turned my back on the log cabin and began walking. I never saw him again.

For years after the war, whenever I met a Russian, I would inquire "Do you know a partisan named Misha?" Of course, Russia being a huge country where almost every other man is called Misha, I never learned anything, though I did come to understand certain things about him and his group. They were Ukrainian partisans resisting the Germans, probably with the help of the Soviet authorities. Some or all of

them may even have been Jewish. The marked differences between them and the Polish partisans were due, in part, to the difference in their circumstances. During the period I knew Misha, the Germans had suffered heavy losses at the hands of the Russians, and the tide of the war was turning against Hitler. This explains the optimism, vigor and relative comfort I found in their camp.

I have always wondered what would have happened had I been able to confide in Misha. However, even with the knowledge I have today, given the same circumstances I believe I would make the same choices: not to speak, not to follow along, not to expose myself to the possibility of violence.

As for Misha I have never forgotten him. Many years later, to keep him always alive in my memory, I gave up "Mishke" and took his name.

She was there! A miracle had happened and there she was, my beautiful mother. "Maman! How did you find me?"

She smiled at me, and I was suffused with the most heavenly bliss.

"Oh, Maman, I'm so happy to see you.

She said something to me but I couldn't hear what it was, and though her lips smiled as she spoke, her eyes did not. Her dark eyes were sad.

"Why are your eyes so sad, Maman?" I asked, but she didn't answer.

It didn't matter. Nothing mattered except that she had

found me and we would be together again. Maman held out her arms to me and I started to run straight into them. My body ached to hug her with all my might, but then I realized with dread that she was beginning to pull away. I tried to catch up with her but my legs wouldn't budge.

"Don't go! Don't go! Please! Wait for me!"

My legs were made of cement! It was so hard... I couldn't move them fast enough. Maman's outstretched arms began to fade, then dissolve into the air.

I woke with a violent jerk. Maman!

I wanted the dream back, but it was gone. I pressed my face against the cold earth and cried.

Alone again. When I met up with Misha's troop I had been walking south for a long time, hoping to pass into some area that was not affected by the war. Now I didn't know which way to go. As usual my thoughts turned to my parents, and I began to feel renewed hope that we would be reunited. If I, a mere child, had survived bombings, executions, freezing cold, starvation, and so many other ordeals, surely my parents, too, had somehow managed to survive. No, they weren't suffering in some ghetto, somewhere; in all probability they were back in Belgium, waiting for me. The more I thought about it, the more certain I became.

It was time to turn back. My only real chance of finding them was in Belgium. I took out my compass and located west. I would not be heading back into the dangers I'd already faced, I'd be returning by a southern route.

Walking toward the afternoon sun, my path felt easier

and my heart lighter. I swung my arms as I ambled along and started to hum to myself: "I'm going to find them, I'm going to find them." My confidence was so high that when I came to a bridge that was guarded by a German soldier I did something I'd never done before. With only a second's hesitation, I strode past, flashed him a bright smile and bounced across the bridge like a child without a care in the world.

CHAPTER 8

Romania
Spring, 1944

CROSSING INTO ROMANIA I ENCOUNTERED increasingly rugged terrain and higher and higher mountains. I had intended to head home by the fastest route—due west—but the Alps blocked my way and forced me to travel south-west, across flatter topography.

I wish I could say that returning homeward my steps were light and my spirit buoyant, but it wasn't so, or rather, not for long. When I made the decision to go back I was full of hope for the first time since the early days of my journey. I hummed to myself as I walked along, imagining how my parents would look, how they might have changed since the last time I saw them. I made lists of all the things I had to remember to tell them, and dreamed about seeing the expression on my mother's face when I told her about the wolves! When I looked back, I thought first of Misha. Each time I remembered him my heart swelled with gratitude. I treasured the knife he gave me, and I'd discovered why its blade was black instead of silver-colored: at night it didn't shine in the moonlight, so it couldn't give you away.

My time with Misha's band had begun to thaw the wall of ice around my heart, and I had let myself feel things that I hadn't felt for so long—a bit of trust in a fellow human, renewed hope that I would be reunited with my parents and a tenuous belief that life might return to normal. But when I opened the door to those feelings, darker emotions that I emotions that I was not expecting, not prepared for, crept in as well. With the passing of time my euphoria wore off and a chronic, nameless malaise settled over me.

In contrast with my darkening mood, the scenery I passed became increasingly glorious. From broad green valleys magnificent granite mountains rose like an anthem high into the cobalt sky, their snowy caps supporting more mountains of billowing white clouds. Like delicate tightrope walkers, wild goats threaded their way along the narrow ridges. At another time, the sight would have filled me with awe, but not now. Now I had other things on my mind.

It began as fleeting moments of melancholy that occurred as I set up my resting place among the stretched out shadows, by the last slanting light of day. As I lay down in my bed, an unspecific sadness, mingled with acute anxiety, would come over me making me feel that I was suffocating. Some nights I would have trouble falling asleep, or I'd awaken at an animal's nocturnal screech and not go back to sleep at all. The next morning I'd rise and head off at first light, but trudging through hilly terrain after a night like that was physically exhausting, and I was beginning to feel as beaten as the walking wraiths I had seen in Warsaw.

On the roads and in the towns there were fewer German soldiers now, but I had noticed men in black uniforms marked with a cross-like insignia. I had no idea who these troops were, friend or foe, just one more possible enemy to avoid. I now surmise they may have been local militia supporting the Germans. One change made my life a bit easier: Though the towns I passed through were war-ravaged and bleak, I was able to find food. I didn't realize at the time that the pressure was lifting from the occupied countries, that the "undefeatable" Germans were now getting close to surrender.

Traveling west, during all my waking hours my mind was fretted by unanswerable questions: How far did I have to go to get home? How long would it take me to get there? Would I really be able to find my parents when I finally arrived? If I'd had any answers, if there had been some limit to the additional suffering I would have to endure before I got home, if I *did* get home, the pain would have been bearable. But for me there was no clear end in sight, so even small struggles that previously I had coped with easily now seemed insurmountable.

Big troubles drove me to the edge of despair. The sight of dead bodies, to which I had become so inured, now became excruciating. The passes across the undulating, verdant foothills of the Alps were littered with hideous corpses in faded striped uniforms, lying singly or in piles next to the road like so much human trash. As spring wildflowers came into bloom, death appeared everywhere; if I didn't see it right away, I knew it by its smell or by a whorl of dark vultures against the brilliant sky. I had hoped never again to witness such atrocity but there it was, at every turn, a bizarre and macabre juxtaposition of horror and beauty. (I later learned how the corpses came to be there: Hitler, anticipating defeat, had organized a series of death marches to speed up the "final solution" and dispose of any remaining Jews.)

Spring came that year and for the first time in my memory I did not rejoice. My body was heavy with weariness, my mind racked with anguish, and I was missing the wolves terribly. They had been my safety, my circle of fire against the evils of the world, and now they were gone. I missed nuzzling my face into their shaggy necks, smelling their fur and feeling their warm bodies pressed against mine. With them gone from my life, I was almost at the end of my rope.

One afternoon, upon finding myself at the bottom of a steeply-rimmed ravine, I looked up at the panoramic sweep of mountains around me and saw only hateful prison walls blocking my route west. How would I ever get myself over the top?

I stood looking at the view a long while before finally steeling myself to start climbing. I still carried with me a fear of heights and there was no help there for the timid climber, no tree limbs or shrubbery to clutch for support, only bare rock. When darkness fell across the steep face of the mountain I slept on the upside of an outcropping of lichen-covered boulders, on a bed of stones. It took me many weeks but eventually I made it to the top of the last high summit.

The wind whipped my hair into my eyes as I stood at the pinnacle looking across rocky peaks and greening valleys, all the way to the horizon. I had to steady myself on a boulder when I peered down the sheer cliffs on the other side—the direction I would have to descend. As I was contemplating my next move, I suddenly thought "Why not stop this torture and just throw yourself over the edge? After all, you'll probably wind up dead like all the other Jews, so why not end it right now?"

I don't know what stopped me, perhaps the glimmer of hope that my parents could be alive. Instead, somehow I managed to find my way down. Still, the temptation to end it all would not go away. Another time when I had to swim across a cold river I heard the same voice urging me "Just plunge your head down, keep it under now—one... two... three... four..." Against my will, my head jerked up and my arms began to churn wildly, propelling me across the current until I hauled myself out on the other side, shivering and gasping with terror.

One night as I lay on my back staring up at the black bowl of the sky strewn with a million winking stars, my mind was like an engine in overdrive. I had suffered so much, I had witnessed suffering far worse than my own, unbelievable suffering inflicted by humans upon their fellows. There was so much capacity for evil in humans. What was the point of it all? Why was I even alive now? To go back, perhaps to suffer more? Perhaps then to die like those children behind me? As if I were watching a movie the whole ghastly scene again began to scroll before my eyes—the truck, the children, the soldiers, the guns; I heard the hammering gunfire and saw the children drop, one by one, in slow motion and, last to fall, the little blond girl holding her doll. Finally the tears came, so hard I thought they would never stop.

When my sobbing subsided I began to think again. In all the time I'd been on my own, with all the miles I'd traveled, the only true happiness I'd discovered, the only real comfort, peace and security, had been with animals, completely outside the realm of human beings. Animals had no capacity for evil, they were pure and innocent. Only with them was I completely free of fear.

Free. In the forest I was as free as the frogs and the beavers and the wolves and I lived in harmony with all of them. How could I give that up and go back to a world of injustice and conflict? Though I began life as a human being, the forest had changed me and now I was no longer human. The only part of my former self that remained was my outside shell, my girl's form. Everything else about me, everything inside, was like an animal's: my reactions, my sensibilities, my very soul. After seeing what human nature was capable of, I wanted no part of my human nature. Yet here I was now, about to reenter the world of human beings. If it took courage to die, it took more to live.

Then at my bleakest moment, I thought of the people who had loved me—my father and mother, and Grandfather whose appearance in my life had come through nothing less than grace, and I thought of the dogs and the wild animals and especially the wolves who had befriended me. The wolves—would they ever be part of my life again or did my going home mean farewell forever? My heart filled with love for them all, I began to breathe deeply and at last I fell asleep.

Until I started heading homeward, I had traveled solely on my own two feet, except for the short jaunt on the stolen bike back in Belgium. But now that I was leaving one life and finding my way toward another, I yearned to be done with wandering and to get on with the future.

I was crossing miles and miles of mountainous territory,

following along the banks of rivers, for I knew that water always takes the easiest route and improves it by carving away the rough places as it flows. But still the going was difficult and my feet protested with pain at every step. The one brief period of relief for me came when I ran across a vender's cart laden with animal pelts on a village street. I quickly snitched a rabbit skin and used it to line the bottom of my boots. That worked well until the weather turned warm. After that I used a square of heavy cloth over each foot, folding it first over the toes and tying it behind my ankles. When I recently explained that device to a friend, she said, "Oh, you made yourself some *chaussettes russes*—'Russian socks.'" They were an improvement but not a remedy.

Though my state of mind was no longer dismal, my physical weariness increased daily. How could I speed up this tedious journey? How could I go farther faster, shortening the days between me and my destination?

One solution came to me as I walked along a country road, and though it was a brief one, at the time it seemed heaven-sent. Across an open field I gazed at a horse so black he seemed to be a silhouette cut from velvet set against a field of emerald green. There were no houses or people nearby so I went up to him and gently ran my fingers down the nape of his neck. I had no food with which to ingratiate myself but I was dying to try to ride him.

It wasn't easy. I'd never mounted a horse before, much less ridden one bare-back. Grasping the wiry mane I managed to pull myself up onto his withers and stay seated. Then, urging him with my voice and my body, I got him to move ahead a bit and even to turn left and right. Fortunately he was a cooperative, gentle beast, but as soon as he began trotting, I slid off and landed with a thud on the ground. I climbed up again and, finally, after some false starts, was able to ride him, my arms around his neck and my knees tightly clutching his sides.

We made it all the way to the end of the village and onto a road that ran along the bank of a river without my once falling off. What's more—and I still can't believe this piece of luck—his owner never caught up with us. A couple of days later, my transportation decided it was time to go home. I ran after him when he took off but, of course, I couldn't catch him. It was no big loss—we hadn't made much headway, but I did enjoy every minute of the adventure.

After that, I began racking my brains for other means of transportation to spare my feet and save time. I was terrified of trains because I had many times seen the long lines of box cars loaded with their doomed human cargo. But what about passenger trains? Whenever I walked along railroad tracks, I wondered if there were any chance of catching a ride. With the language barrier, no money to buy a ticket and no identification, it would be impossible to board one at a depot like an ordinary passenger. And of course there would be German soldiers at all the stations and on the trains. But perhaps I could stow away somehow.

Once I'd seen two filthy children crawl out from under a train just as it came to a stop. They'd obviously latched on to something underneath. If they could do it, why couldn't I? I kept my eyes open around train stations, always watching from a distance, but it took a while for me to find the right opportunity.

Finally, I got my chance. Very early one morning, just a little after daybreak, as I was following the rails westward I arrived at a depot. Two or three people were waiting on the platform, pacing up and down impatiently. After a while I heard the polyphonic wail of a train whistle in the east, and watched as a long trail of white smoke wafted above the trees and an engine nosed into sight from around the bend.

The train slowed as it approached the station and by the time it halted, I had positioned myself just behind the last car. I stepped between the tracks and looked around. Could anyone see me from the platform? No! I quickly kneeled down and peered under the car. Between the sets of gleaming steel wheels a long plank was suspended from the car's underbelly. That must be where one rides, I decided. I crawled under the train and slid my body onto the plank, face down. Just then the conductor shouted and the train hissed loudly and started to jerk forward. With a mix of fear and elation I grabbed the plank with both arms and hung on for dear life.

The ride was far worse than anything I could ever have anticipated. As soon as the train began to pick up speed I doubted I would be able to hold on. Bits of rubble pelted my face, and no matter how tightly I squeezed them shut, dirt blew into my eyes and mouth. I was jolted and jostled so violently as the train sped along that I feared my body would burst like a big egg, shattering every nerve, spilling my guts onto the tracks. I was in terror that one sudden lurch of that fiendish locomotive would snap my iron grip on the plank and I'd be ground to sausage meat under the wheels. As if all that weren't enough, when we entered a tunnel the train whistle began to shriek hellishly and so it continued until we finally came out the other side, whereupon a blast of hot wind blew all the grime in the universe into my face.

Somehow, I managed to hold on until we reached a station. The instant the train came to a stop I slid off the plank and crawled out onto the rails. On trembling legs I bolted from the depot. Spitting grit out of my mouth as I ran, I came to a deserted place where I threw myself down and rolled over and over in the grass trying to rub off the black soot that clung to me everywhere. I would never try that means of travel again.

But I continued to follow the tracks because they took the easiest route across hilly terrain. Sometime later another kind of train ride worked to perfection for me, saving me many long miles of walking. One morning, as I was approaching a range of steep hills, smoke rising from the engine of a stationary line of open cattle cars drew me closer to have a look.

Up front two trainmen were standing in a cloud of steam, their heads together, shouting over the hissing of the engine. I crossed the tracks behind the last car and looked in all directions. There was no one watching. Placing one foot on the hub of a big wheel I pulled myself up by the horizontal planks that supported the bales of hay, then hoisted myself over the top rail and dropped into the open car. As I snuggled down out of sight between the bales I could hear cattle mooing up the line.

The engine breathed a loud hiss, the wheels squealed and we began to move ahead. As soon as the train had gone a few yards I popped up my head and peered out. It was a wonderful ride. Hills, farms and winding roads were flowing by me in a continuous stream. Horses and wagons, sheep and an occasional cow appeared, then trailed off into distant specks. We climbed the steep hills and came down again, so easily, so effortlessly, and all I had to do was lie there, resting in the hay.

When the train pulled into a stop and I heard men's voices on the platform, I ducked down between the bales and waited, desperately hoping they wouldn't come to my car. Fortunately, they never did. After some minutes the train lurched forward, and again I watched the miles streak by, lulled by the rhythmic throbbing of the wheels and the gentle swaying of the car. Eventually the train arrived at its destination and stock yard workers began unloading cattle from the front cars. My train ride was over; I jumped to the ground and regretfully continued on foot.

Yugoslavia
Summer, 1944

The landscape had changed dramatically. The river I was following had turned brackish and now I came across mussels growing on jetties along the bank, a tasty meal, there for the picking. Seagulls and kingfishers plied the estuaries and the air smelled of salt marsh and fish. Finally I came to a harbor (in the city of Dubrovnik, I later determined) and I knew I could go no farther—I had come to the sea. I slept on, or near, the main pier for several days trying to figure out what to do next.

Obviously, if I were to continue going west it would have to be by boat, so each day I studied the traffic in the little harbor. Well before dawn the fishing boats set out to sea, returning with their catch in the afternoon. Occasionally a fisherman would notice me watching from the dock as the catch was unloaded and toss me a handful of sardines. I also ate oysters that grew in beds near the pier, breaking them open with a rock.

On several evenings I noticed a motor boat taking on passengers and heading out across the water. Where were they going? At night as I lay curled up under a crate on the pier I once or twice heard the low murmur of voices, then a motor starting up, humming briefly and fading in the distance. I was too tired to get up to look but in the morning I thought about what I'd heard. There were all kinds of surreptitious comings and goings from the pier, but I had no idea how find out who was transporting whom to where, and no hope of being included.

One afternoon as I sat tired and alone on the wharf, dangling my legs over the water and envying the gulls their apparently effortless means of transportation, a middle-aged couple arrived, carrying small suitcases. They spoke in low tones and seemed a bit lost. After a while the couple came up to me and asked me something in a language I didn't understand. I just shrugged and looked away.

The ocean was a sheet of polished copper reflecting the setting sun, and in the distance I could see the thin, silver wake of a boat heading into port. The woman touched my shoulder, nodded toward the boat, and questioned me again in a different language. "Comacchio? Comacchio?" she kept repeating. Still I looked at her blankly.

Then: "Italia?"

Suddenly I understood! Italy! That boat was going to Italy! The Italy on Grandfather's map, shaped like a boot and right next to France, which was right next to my own Belgium. If that's where it was headed, all I had to do was get on board.

All I had to do—yes, but how? I had no papers, no money and the boat looked to be too small for me to stow away. Once again I shook my head at the woman. No, I didn't understand.

The boat drew alongside and moored at the dock. It was small and sturdy, like a tug boat, and painted black and white, with an pilot house atop and room below for passengers. As the skipper disembarked, two or three other people began walking down the pier to meet him, and soon they and the first couple were all conferring with him in whispers. I strained my ears to catch a word or two of their conversation. If they were indeed about to become passengers bound for Italy, I desperately yearned to do the same. My mind was going a mile a minute trying to figure how I could get on such a boat.

A young, very blonde woman I hadn't noticed before walked by me. As she passed, she looked at me curiously as though she, too, wanted to ask me something. I looked away and she continued on, toward the group at the end of the pier, where she waited until all the others had finished with the captain. Then I saw her approach him and offer a small package she took from her shoulder bag. They seemed to be doing business. From my perch I couldn't tell what she was holding, something small, perhaps a piece of jewelry. Then she turned around and glanced at me. I quickly averted my eyes, pretending that I hadn't been paying attention to her.

A few minutes later she walked over to where I was sitting, bent down and spoke to me. All I could think was, "That's the second woman questioning me in a language I don't understand." Once again I shook my head, and once again another language replaced the first. But this time I understood.

"Tu comprends le français?"

I nodded "Yes, I understand."

"Look," she said in heavily accented French, "That boat's leaving for Italy in a little while."

I looked at her blankly. What did that have to do with me?

"I'm going to Italy. Would you like to come with me?"

What?! Did she actually say that? It didn't seem possible. Go to Italy! Get out of there and be miraculously transported to within a stone's throw of my destination! I couldn't believe such luck. Yet at the same time I was hesitant. To accept the invitation would mean having to be with a person, linking myself to a human being.

Seeing my hesitation, she continued: "I'm blonde, you're blonde, you could pass for my daughter. It would be easy."

What could I do? There was no other way. I was too tired to resist and there might not be another opportunity. I had to take the risk.

I slowly nodded "Yes."

The woman told me her name was Liane and asked me mine, but when I made my mute gestures she inquired no more. Instead, she walked back to the skipper, pointed in my direction and gave him something else from her little package. Then as the sun dropped into the sea we were all led aboard, across the deck and down a short flight of steps to our seats below. Six of us crammed ourselves together on hard wooden benches. There in the dark we waited... and waited... and waited. The delay was endless. Now and then the silence was broken by terse whispers from the others who seemed as anxious to get moving as I.

By the time the boat finally cast off and set out into the harbor I was feeling as anxious as a trapped animal so I left my seat and went up on deck where I could breath sea air, away from people. I leaned my elbows on the rail and looked out over the water. We were chugging slowly along the shoreline. I watched the stone walls of the city in the moonlight, gradually shrinking and fading in the distance, and wondered what awaited me when we landed.

We seemed to be running along the coastline, weaving our way through small islands, and I began to worry that we weren't heading for Italy after all. In a little while the skipper signaled me to go below. It was dark in the cabin for we were running without lights. I took my seat next to the woman who called herself Liane and pressed my nose against the grimy window. Despite the full moon I couldn't see much of anything because waves constantly washed across the glass.

In the darkness I heard the sound of paper crumpling as Liane took a packet out of her purse, opened it and handed me a half of a large roll filled with cheese. Then she left me for a moment and came back with two small containers of water. After that, I remember very little because I slept almost the whole trip, crumpled next to Liane, my head against the window.

Around sunrise I opened my eyes and saw her watching me.

"You can talk," she said.

I looked at her, bewildered.

"You spoke in your sleep. In French. So you can talk, can't you?"

I answered "Oui"—my first word spoken to a human being since I ran away.

We traveled the rest of the way in silence. When I got up to use the toilet, a nasty little hole that made me long for the woods, I went up on deck again and saw with relief that the shore was receding behind us and we were headed out into open water and across the Adriatic Sea. I returned to my place and immediately fell asleep again, scarcely waking until evening when we reached the port of Comacchio on the northeastern coast of Italy. We disembarked in darkness. As we stood on the dock Liane gently took my hand.

"Come with me," she whispered.

But my old angels of mistrust held me back and I shook my head "No." She studied me with a worried smile then shrugged her shoulders, as if to say "Well, I tried." When she turned and walked off I headed the other way.

By an extraordinary coincidence, I would run into Liane in Belgium many years later. I learned then that she was a Romanian Jew who recognized herself in the blonde ragamuffin she spotted on the Dubrovnik pier. She, too, had been a tired wanderer only a short time before.

At the time I boarded the boat with Liane, the Allies were winning the war. On the Eastern Front the Russians had made great gains, liberating territory after territory from the Nazis. By 1944 plans were underway for the Allied invasion of Europe under joint American and British command. At 1:30 a.m. on June 6, 1944 ("D-Day"), American troops landed at Normandy on the coast of France and, despite heavy losses, began pushing north toward Germany. The Russians under commanders Zhukov and Konev would soon lay siege to Berlin, the heart of the Third Reich. Although Hitler's fate was sealed much earlier, Germany would finally capitulate on May 8, 1945 and four months later the Allies would celebrate their victory over Japan. The Second World War would be over.

Long before then I would be back in Belgium.

Italy
Autumn, 1944

NO SUN, JUST DREARY DRIZZLE alternating with savage downpours, puddles like ponds, streams wide as rivers, acres of mud—that was the welcome awaiting me in Italy that fall. The rolling green hills of the Italian countryside were pockmarked, scorched and deeply scarred. Roads disappeared into rubble-filled gulches, bridges collapsed into rivers, junk piles of destroyed artillery lay rusting in puddles of rain.

Occasionally I'd hear over the hammering of the rain the sound of bombs or cannon fire in the distance, but in spite of the weather and the war, I managed to get along. Whenever the downpour let up a bit, I slept in the open under felled trees gnarled and blackened by artillery fire. In deserted villages I holed up in gutted buildings with pigeons fluttering in the rafters and the stench of moisture leaching through charred walls.

The countryside held opportunities as well as grim reminders—farms, barns and crops in the fields. When I arrived in the villages, I encountered other children who appeared to be war orphans like me, scrounging in the streets, barefoot and bedraggled. There were so many of them begging on the street, I did the same, just another casualty holding out my hand for food.

After leaving Liane I had set my sights northwest, trying to keep as much as possible to flat areas and following the rivers as was my custom. The mild weather afforded me the luxury of bathing more frequently. That's not to say that everything was fine—I was still a homeless wanderer. But Belgium and the end of the journey was so much closer that excitement and hope eased my fatigue and propelled me forward.

I was far less frightened now than I'd been before because there were few Germans about. In many areas I observed new kinds of soldiers, in uniforms I'd never seen before. These seemed to be spirited young men who were warmly welcomed by the townsfolk. I saw villagers helping to push their military jeeps when they got mired in the sea of mud, and sometimes the local ladies bestowed flowers and kisses upon them. As the distance narrowed between me and my homeland, my confidence expanded. I felt that nothing could stop me now, there was no obstacle I couldn't overcome.

Did I talk to people yet? No, because I couldn't—I didn't speak or understand Italian. Besides, I had gotten along very well as a mute, and there seemed no reason to throw aside the mistrust that had protected me for so long. Occasionally I was offered a ride in an automobile, which I always declined, but I very willingly climbed into horse-drawn wagons when local peasants offered me a lift.

There were still a handful of Germans left around. In a remote, nearly-deserted village I remember seeing a couple of soldiers riding a motorcycle, one driving, the other in a side-car. As they passed me the driver accidentally dropped something and braked to a stop. He called out to me over his shoulder, his motor still running, and it was obvious he

The earliest pictures I
have of myself as a child
(age 7), taken at the
"Polyphoto" shop when
I was given my new
identity.

Here is Grandfather

...and this is Marthe.

Grandfather, Marthe and Ita.

Marthe and me
with my new doll,
on the day of our
big outing.

The canal (Canal de Charleroi) on the outskirts of Brussels that I crossed when I ran away.

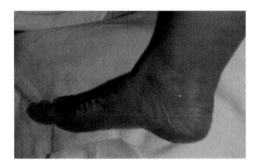

1983. I had surgery on my feet to correct deformities caused by years of walking and bad shoes.

The little compass Grandfather gave me. I have it to this day.

A village in the Ardennes.

A shack in the Belgium woods.

Me, at age 30, with
dyed hair—black, in
memory of my mother.
I still looked young for
my age.

Me in 1975. I
like this picture.
On my face you
can still see the
anger.

1979. Me with my husband and my son (age 17) on a vacation in Arizona several years before we moved to America.

1981. With my husband, Maurice, in Holland. Finally, my face looks happy.

Me at age 40.
My love of animals
expressed through my
passion for clothes.

This is me in a
Russian-style hat
I still own, with
Gamin who died
in 1995. The brim
is decorated with
brass stars I picked
off a dead soldier.

wanted me to pick it up and hand it to him. I just pretended I didn't understand and walked away, thinking, "I'm not afraid of you, *boche*, I killed one just like you."

Just before I left Italy and crossed into France, something quite wonderful happened to me. On a street corner one bright, sunny day, I came across a group of four or five uniformed young men, not yet out of their teens, joking and laughing exuberantly. As I walked by I studied them curiously from the corner of my eye. They were foreigners, speaking a language I didn't recognize, but dressed like others who were welcomed in the villages. They behaved differently from the rough and rowdy Russian soldiers I'd come across, and completely unlike the pompous Germans. These soldiers seemed so pleasant, so natural; there was something childlike and appealing in their manner and the way they kidded around with each other.

As I passed them, one of the group waved his hand and called me over. He was very tall and strikingly handsome, with a wide, friendly grin and he wore his cap pushed way back on his head. I hesitated only a moment before deciding it would be safe to approach. They all began talking to me at once, smiling and gesturing to make me understand. I just stood there smiling too, but obviously not understanding a word. Then, at one point, one jabbed a thumb in his chest and said, "American! *Americano?*"

Of course I understood the word from "*Américain*" in French. One of them took a small can out of a case, opened it, and held it out to show me. I smelled it. It was some kind of meat that he wanted me to taste. I'd never seen food like that, much less eaten it. The soldier kept repeating "monkey meat, monkey meat" and the others laughed, but I quickly took him up on his offer. "Monquimite!" I repeated the funny sounding name to myself as I polished it off, storing the word in my memory. Later I figured out my canned treat was Spam or corned beef, the usual army rations, but a real luxury for me.

When I'd finished, the tall one squatted down next to me, unwrapped a bar of chocolate and gave me the whole thing. I wanted to save part of it for later but he kept urging me to eat it all. Then he twisted the candy wrapper into a pair of wings like the silver insignia on his uniform and gave it to me. And here is the most wonderful part: As I finished the candy he scooped me up and sat me on his knees.

I don't understand what happened to me at that moment. Suddenly all of my mistrust dissolved. From head to toe every cell of my body seemed to burst into a smile; it was a moment out of time. I felt like a princess on a throne, so special, so singled out. Surely my father must have taken me on his lap like that when I was very little, but I had no memory of it. Now, as my flyer sat there joking with his buddies, one hand on my shoulder, I turned my head to peek at his face—a boy's face with smooth skin, gray-blue eyes the color of the morning sky, and a cherub's mouth from which emanated the most disarming laugh I'd ever heard. I have no idea how long I sat there on his knees, it may have been ten minutes or only one, but for as long as it lasted I was in heaven.

France
Winter, 1945

Just over the border into French territory, I stole a bicycle and managed to travel quite a few miles northward before it broke down. I was so anxious to get home that I'd wake in the dark at the hour of nature's changing of the guard, when the nightingales gave way to the larks, and watch the sun come up as I walked along. Whenever I could, I'd improve my progress by hitching rides in wagons that were going my way.

For the first time in years, I was in a country where people spoke my language, and I began to speak to those who greeted me or asked me questions. It wasn't a conscious decision; it just seemed the natural thing to do. When someone driving a cart spotted me and yelled in French, "Hey, *petite*, want a lift?" I'd answer, "*Oui, monsieur, merci, monsieur*" and hop on. And if anyone asked where my parents were, I'd say "Up north"—"*au nord*"—and they'd go out of their way a little to take me in the right direction. We would often chat a bit on these rides. My fellow travelers were more than friendly and helpful, they were in high spirits, elated, giddy, buoyant. As I was now able to converse, I soon came to understand the reason why: France's own army had recently routed the Germans from Paris. France was free! Now, though the Nazis had not surrendered, everyone sensed that the end was near.

It was good to be able to speak again. Today people sometimes ask me if it was strange or difficult when I first began, but the truth is I never really stopped. During my travels I always spoke to animals, birds, bugs and snakes and even flowers and trees, so I was comfortable right away answering sociable questions and asking directions.

No, for me, the most difficult problem was my increasing ambivalence. As the weather became colder I could see lamps shining in the windows of warm houses. Then the free me, the wild me, the me who had been so content in the forest and proud to eke out survival on her own terms, began to tire of independence and of a life lacking in the most basic comforts. I thought wistfully, enviously, of farmers warming themselves by a wood stove. Or even better, of people like La DeWael with her modern central heating, her furnace fired by a huge pile of coal left by a delivery man.

The soul of an animal; the body and desires of a human being—that was me. How I hated to give up the animal in me! And at the same time how I longed to have what other human beings had. Perhaps I'd already realized that insatiable need to have it all or anticipated it when I told Grandfather "I want the moon" and—after he pretended to give it to me—demanded another one.

Along with these contradictions another big one nagged at me. My old rule of never trusting human beings had saved my life and although I was speaking to people now, the iron wall of mistrust I'd erected around myself was by no means down. But how could I reconcile that wall with the kindness shown to me by Misha, or Liane's spontaneous generosity; or the friendliness of the American soldier who held me so sweetly on his lap?

This lonely child was in need of more warmth than all of La DeWael's burning coal could provide.

From a distance I had expected low hills, but once I reached the top of the first one, another slope faced me, steeper and longer than the first, then still another. It was too late now to turn back and look for a more level route, so I pushed onward and upward, hoping for a last summit and smooth passage down. The higher I climbed, the foggier it became, until soon the mist was so thick I could barely see the trees around me.

Then there emerged from the fog, on a peak just ahead of me, a high stone edifice, like an old fairy tale castle with towers and turrets and tall, narrow windows. Low along the front there seemed to be a wall, before which several white forms were bobbing slowly up and down in the mist. What were they? I walked closer and, when I arrived at the gate, finally was able to distinguished the wide-winged, white bonnets of several nuns who were bent over among the tidy rows of a budding vegetable garden. Food! There was food there—and perhaps a warm fire inside.

I followed a stone path that led to a massive door of carved wood with iron straps and a huge iron knocker. This seemed to be a convent. Perhaps, in their mercy, the sisters would not only feed me but also let me stay the night. Why not give it a try? I thought to myself.

I lifted the knocker, letting it drop with a resounding whack, and immediately saw all the bonnets in the garden lift as the sisters looked my way. After a long while the door was opened by a rosy-cheeked nun in a long gray habit, with a thick chain around her waist from which hung a set of large brass keys. "*Oui, mon enfant?*" she said gently, "Why have you come?" I was hungry and was hoping I might have something to eat, I explained. Without hesitating or asking any questions, she motioned me to enter.

A long hall led to a large open room, unheated but not uncomfortably cold, with dark wooden beams overhead and Gothic windows. The stone floor was covered with straw beds and on them sat a dozen or more bedraggled little boys. They took no notice of me but continued chatting together like old comrades.

The nun instructed me to wait there and disappeared through a heavy wooden door. I squatted down in the corner and looked around. The room was plain and sparsely furnished save for several framed depictions of holy figures that hung along the walls. My eyes lingered on one of beautiful winged creatures with floating robes and serene faces, a host of heavenly angels that reminded me of the gauzy figures in the picture in Grandfather's home.

The ragamuffins on the straw drew my attention and I strained to hear their conversation. I gathered that they were battle-scarred war orphans and homeless castaways being sheltered in this remote abbey. Soon the sister returned with bread and a bowl of warm milk. I ate slowly, hoping she would not expect me to leave when I'd finished. By now dusk was gathering outside the leaded windowpanes. My belly full, I rested my head on the straw and immediately fell asleep.

Hours later, or perhaps only minutes, through my somnolent haze there came to my ears a tune carried by a quavering soprano voice. Another joined in, and another, then a chorus of little boys' voices raised in song. At first I thought I was dreaming, but the music went on, and in it was imbued all the innocence of all the children who ever had suffered the insufferable horrors of war. As I listened with my eyes closed, I swallowed hard and tears wet the straw under my head.

> Here we know but one purpose
> and each of us plays his part,
> Friend, if you fall, from the shadows
> another will take your place.
> Tomorrow the hot sun will sear away
> the bloodshed on the highway,
> Comrades sing out, for in the night
> Liberty is listening.

> *Içi, chacun sait ce qu'il veut,*
> *ce qu'il fait quand il passe,*
> *Ami, si tu tombes, un ami*
> *sort de l'ombre à ta place,*
> *Demain du sang noir sèchera*
> *au grand soliel sur le routes,*
> *Chantez compagnons, dans la nuit*
> *la Liberté nous écoute.*

There came another verse, and another and I was borne away to a place where there was no pain. If indeed there were angels in a heaven somewhere far from man's sordid realm, surely they would sound like this.

What I heard that evening was *Le Chant de la Libération* of the French partisans, which even today brings tears to my eyes.

Belgium
Spring, 1945

It was easy to tell I was in Belgium. Even if I hadn't recognized the Belgian accent, the style of the houses or the familiar dress of the peasants, I certainly recognized the name on the sign, "La Louviere." So there I was. And there, with any luck, the two people I had been dreaming of for so long would be waiting for me.

But how could we find each other? They must already have been searching for me in all the likely places. I couldn't imagine how to locate them myself. I wouldn't walk into the police station and make inquiries—my sense of danger had hardly abated enough for that.

It didn't seem possible that Maman and Papa would have returned to that gloomy hideout in Schaerbeek, the place where they'd been arrested, and anyway, try as I might, I couldn't remember where it was or the name of our street. The only detail that came to mind was the tram I left on: number 56. There might be a way of finding it, following it to the street we'd lived on, though I recalled it made turns along the way.

When I saw the first sign for Brussels my heart skipped a beat and my pace quickened. Several days later I arrived within sight of the canal then came to the very bridge I'd crossed the morning after my escape. That was my first real ray of hope. Finally, I was certain I could find my way to Grandfather's farm.

Grandfather and Marthe—A bed! Food and warm clothes! At last, safety! And they could help me find my parents. But would they remember me? Would they even recognize me, the way I looked now? All the destruction I'd seen made me afraid to hope, yet hope I did that the nightmare soon would be over. I started on the familiar path through the fields, recognizing the little stone church, the houses, all the landmarks that had greeted me so long ago on my visits to Grandfather's farm. My heart beat faster. What would they look like? What would they say when they saw me. Did they still have Rita and Ita? My feet couldn't walk fast enough for me and I began to run.

Then I stopped and froze in horror. There, where I used to take the lane that led to the farm, stood, not farmhouses with carefully tended fields and meadows of sheep and cows, but—nothing. I turned my head in all directions. The whole area was an empty desert of scrub and stones and weeds. The houses, the barns, the fences, the animals, everything had disappeared. My eyes full of tears, I stumbled on, thinking that I must ask Grandfather what had happened to the neighbors' farms. Finally, in the distance I recognized the silhouette of the big walnut tree that marked the boundary of Grandfather's farm, and just behind it, where the hen house had sheltered my *coucou de Malines*, I could see— nothing. All trace of the farmhouse, the orchard, the barn, the animals, Grandfather and Marthe—gone.

Again! Again! I cried to myself. Just once, couldn't one good thing happen for me? Couldn't one thing turn out right?

The street market in my home town was noisy and bustling with people but as usual I was all alone, trying to figure out how to get by. Where could I turn to find out what had happened to Grandfather and Marthe? The authorities? Who were they? Where were they? And anyway, I was terrified of any kind of authority. I ambled through the crowd, examining the stalls on either side of me, their canvas awnings flapping in the wind. The displays of old clothes and handmade crafts didn't interest me, but not far from the butcher shop was a produce stand. Unfortunately the vendor, a plump red-faced woman, had eyes on all sides of her head. I knew that because she'd yelled at me the week before when I tried to pocket an apple, and I'd bolted out of the market, grabbing items from every stall I passed and upsetting carts on my way.

Now I headed for a more promising stall where the man in charge was busy haggling with a housewife over the price of potatoes. My knapsack could use a carrot or two on top of what I'd already filched. As I approached the stand, I felt a tap on my shoulder and heard a voice behind me:

"What have you got there? I turned around to see a tall, blond boy standing behind me. He looked to be about 17 years old, and he was staring hard at me.

"In your bag. What have you got there?"

I paused a moment, then answered, "Nothing."

"Yes you do have something. I saw you. You took stuff."

I shook my head and started to walk away, but the boy walked right along with me. "You'd be better off to hand it over to me."

Did this jerk think he had a right to my food? I would

stall him until we reached a crowd of people up ahead, then give him the slip.

"Why should I?"

"You'd be better off pooling it with us."

I kept on walking. "Who's us?"

"Our gang. We have a gang and we pool everything we get. That way each one gets more. It makes more sense."

We were almost up to the crowd. The boy continued talking, while I tried to figure how to lose him. I'd do it just beyond that next stall. He'd attract too much attention if he tried to chase me. What had he just said?

"We have this house..."

A house!

"We found it. It was empty so we took it over."

Now I was listening!

It was a white stone house on a dirt road in the country, surrounded by tall straggly bushes. Its flat roof was edged with a low stone balustrade, and all the windows were tightly shuttered.

Sigui, as he introduced himself to me, led me to a window around the side (the front door was locked when they took it over, he explained, and they had no key) and hoisted me inside. Except for slender ribbons of sunlight filtering through slits in the shutters, the room was dark and unfurnished. Grimy cushions and blankets were strewn all over the floor and spider webs, not curtains, adorned the windows. Sigui climbed through the window and joined me inside.

"Where would I sleep?"

"There," he said, pointing to the grimy cushions on the floor.

On one of them I made out the shaggy head of a sleeping boy.

"That's Gorilla—Felix the Gorilla. C'mon, I'll show you the house."

There was no heat, electricity or working plumbing but instead burnt stubs of candles everywhere and quite a few basins and buckets—used for transporting water from a well to the house, Sigui explained.

He led me to a large kitchen and, just beyond, an impressive pantry stocked with bread, apples, dried beans and other edibles. Fully convinced now, I reached into my knapsack, pulled out my items of food, and deposited them on the kitchen table. Sigui gave a brief nod of approval.

"Let's go," he said. "We have to meet the others at the plateau."

I followed him out the window. We walked for a mile or so to a high hill near a woods and stopped at the top in a wide flat clearing, the area Sigui had called the "plateau," his gang's rendezvous.

It was a handy spot where they all convened at the end of a day of acquiring food and supplies, before heading on back to the house. From the summit you could look down and see if you were being followed or if any police were around. If anything below looked suspicious, you could scoot down the back side of the hill and hide in the woods.

Sigui told me that the police could be a problem. Neighbors on the other side of their house were upset that a bunch of young squatters, vagabonds and punks had taken the place over, and they regularly called the police station to complain. Sigui explained that sometimes, when there was trouble in the area, one or two of the group climbed a stairway to the roof and kept watch. One whistle and everyone jumped out the window and scattered into the woods.

One by one, members of the gang arrived at the plateau and Sigui introduced me to them. They were teenagers, all older than me. (I was not yet twelve at the time.) Sigui, the eldest, was obviously the chief. He seemed to be the only boy there without a colorful nickname. One gang member was a square-faced fellow called "the Canadian," though he was, in fact, French. Out of admiration for the Canadian troops who had liberated his village, he hoped one day to settle in that far-off land. And I'd already seen "Felix the Gorilla," simian-faced and a bit of a buffoon, he spoke French with a Polish accent. Now Sigui was introducing me to someone they called "Lamb."

Lamb must have been about fourteen or fifteen years old. He was fine-featured, slender, with pale, almost transparent, skin, long delicate fingers and jet black hair. He seemed sad and painfully shy; when I said "Hello" to him, he barely answered. The Canadian, who had taken the meek boy under his wing, explained that before Lamb had been rescued by the Red army, his mother and father were murdered by Nazis right before his eyes. The Canadian tapped the side of his head with his finger to tell me that Lamb was not all there upstairs, but something about the boy immediately appealed to me.

There were girls in the group, too. One whose name I can't remember was a thin brunette with rabbit teeth. Another, Margot, had thick, red hair and large breasts. According to one of the boys, she had a lot of what the Yanks called "le sex appeal." Thanks to Margot's flirtation with a neighboring farmer, the gang was often treated to warm, home-cooked meals.

I gradually settled into the communal life. We were all homeless strays and, although the war had affected each of us in different ways, we all had been scarred and changed by it. It was a blessed feeling of security to sleep in a real house and to have the camaraderie and protection of the group. The only bullets and bombs I faced were those in my nightmares. Not that I became sweet and docile by any means. After four years on my own, living like a wild animal, a mere house and companions couldn't domesticate me.

I was still a tomboy. If the boys threw knives at targets for sport, I competed too. If they wrestled, I did too. Though I was much smaller than all of them I could always hold my own. Once, when the Canadian was unable to wrestle me to the ground, he said, "That's no fair. You're using willpower!"

Because of my bullish behavior, I myself wound up with a nickname: "Buffalo." I was proud of it.

Under Sigui's leadership the gang was well organized. We would take turns going on stealing forays, usually working in teams of two, especially on Tuesdays, the day of the local street market where I first ran into Sigui. There seemed to be no end to the goods we acquired: every sort of food imaginable, cushions to sleep on, even regulation army sleeping bags and, most impressive of all, somebody's fine bicycle, now the property of the Canadian. We had a swaggering bravado and a "one-for-all, all-for-one" spirit that made anything seem possible.

The only boy in the group who didn't roughhouse or go out stealing was Lamb. He could sit quietly for hours, staring into space with a look of wistful melancholy. The others accepted him and let him be. I was drawn to Lamb and liked to walk with him or just sit by his side, dreaming along with him. Neither of us would say a word, but I sensed he liked having me there beside him.

I began to look forward more and more to seeing Lamb and spending time with him. When we were together I became suffused with a kind of glow and my pulse raced. My feelings for him must have shone in my eyes, because a couple of times I noticed one of the gang pointing at us, smiling or nudging someone, as if to say, "Oh-oh. Somebody's got a bountje" (a crush.)

I could tell that Lamb felt it too. Then one day, as we sat on the edge of a wall with our feet dangling down, our hands happened to brush, and somehow, as if on signal, our fingers interlaced. Our hands remained clasped for a long time, and from that joining an extraordinary feeling, one I had never experienced before, welled up in me. Lamb was my first love.

It didn't occur to me that other girls in the group might have had such feelings. Most of the time all the kids behaved like a family or like old, familiar comrades, joking and fighting. We slept in close quarters but there were no physical gestures of affection between us or sexual advances of any kind.

The only time I had any idea of such matters was the night I heard soft laughter in the next room. Most of the gang were asleep, and I was lying on a couple of old cushions, half dreaming, when I became aware of two voices softly humming a tune I recognized as one the Yanks listened to on the radio, "Moonlight Serenade," then more muted laughter and whispers. I got up on my elbow and peered into the darkness—who was moving around in the next room?

I quietly rose, tiptoed to the doorway and then stopped abruptly and watched. The shutters had been opened and moonlight poured in through the dusty windows. In each corner of the room candles flickered. Silhouetted in a pool of silver light, Sigui was dancing with Margot, holding her so tight their long shadows merged on the peeling walls. They were humming the dance tune and slowly rocking back and forth to their own music, their heads together, his arms around her waist and hers around his neck. Then, as they continued to dance, she lifted her face to his and they kissed—a kiss that seemed to go on and on forever.

I had never seen anything like that, a boy and a girl kissing. It was a revelation to me—strange, romantic, overwhelming. I could only stand there and gape. Then suddenly I hiccuped and Sigui turned and caught a glimpse of me open-mouthed, eyes wide as saucers, and he began to laugh. I dove back into my bed, grateful for the darkness, as I was blushing furiously. Later with Sigui and Margot I pretended that none of this had ever happened.

With the passage of time, I began to understand more

and more about what was going on in the world beyond our squatters' domain. Every night by candlelight we would all sit on the floor in the big front room, and the gang members—mostly the older ones—would tell fascinating stories about their experiences before coming to the big house. Most of them had been orphaned by the war and had traveled long distances—a few were from Poland, others from Czechoslovakia or Russia. Some of them had found themselves in the thick of military battles which they described with great relish and had come to Brussels after the city was liberated by the British the previous September. Young as they were, they knew a lot about the important events of the war. The Canadian, for example, explained to me that the Soviet forces right then were advancing toward Hitler's headquarters in Berlin, and when they got there the war would be over.

And soon afterwards it happened—the war in Europe ended. Germany surrendered unconditionally, Hitler was dead and Belgium celebrated victory in Europe on May 8, 1945—VE-Day. Church bells rang, the Belgian flag waved everywhere, confetti and streamers flew out of windows, truckloads of Allied soldiers rolled down the streets and the Belgian people, wild with joy, embraced each other.

Sigui boosted me up on a windowsill so that I could see over the madly cheering crowd. I was not impressed. The end of the war meant one less worry for me, but it didn't bring me joy. I could only think: *they* are happy but I'm not. The war is over, great! but I've lost my parents. Living in the abandoned house I was unable even to go to the town hall to try to find out what happened to them. If someone there asked me where I lived or what I did, what could I say? "I am a squatter in that house full of hooligans and I live by stealing?" And how could anyone help me when I didn't even know what name to ask for?

Not long afterwards, though, my life did take a turn in a radically new direction. I was walking back to the house alone late one afternoon. I had gone up to the plateau to rendezvous with the others and show them some articles I'd stolen, but, to my surprise, no one was there. I thought perhaps I'd arrived too late, so I headed for home by myself. As I trudged up the dirt road to the house, I saw Sigui running toward me.

"Don't go in there!" he shouted. "Stay where you are. I'll be right back." Then he ran back to the house.

What was going on? Was it the police? No, it couldn't be, because then Sigui wouldn't have gone back. I couldn't imagine what was happening, but I waited in the road as I'd been told. Why couldn't I go in the house? If there was trouble perhaps I could help. I sat on the ground and impatiently studied the house.

After a long time the window opened and Sigui appeared. Closing it behind him he walked slowly down the lane to where I was waiting. The look on his face told me immediately something was terribly wrong. He stood stiffly before me and started to speak but at first couldn't get his words out. Finally he blurted out the terrible news:

"Lamb is dead."

"What?!"

"He's dead. He hanged himself."

No! It wasn't possible. I was stunned, but the news

didn't really register. Lamb dead? How could that be? I was with him just hours ago. I started to walk toward the house but Sigui wouldn't let me go. He knew I'd seen death hundreds of times, but this was different. Lamb was my friend.

Again he told me to wait while he returned to the house. I stood outside the house, silent tears running down my cheeks, watching and waiting, but nobody else came out to speak with me. Inside, they were trying to figure out what to do with the body, how to dispose of it, the Canadian would explain to me later.

In the distance I heard a siren growing louder and louder. A black police van pulled up in front of the house and two policeman got out. After that, everything happened so fast I didn't have time to grieve.

Not one member of the gang ever considered running away. With Lamb's suicide everything changed; our proud independence, our cocky self-sufficiency instantly crumbled. Our collective spirit was broken. It was as though a living body had given up with the collapse of one small but vital organ. Without actually saying or thinking it consciously, we all had given up.

The police took us to headquarters and questioned us, one by one: Who were we? What were we doing in the house? Did we have any family? How long had we been there?—and so on. One of the neighbors apparently had noticed something amiss and alerted the authorities. The officers themselves weren't so bad. They treated us considerately, even sympathetically, in fact. After we'd been there a while they brought us cold cuts and cheese and hot chocolate.

I was interviewed by an Officer Martens, a gray-haired, avuncular policeman who told me that the authorities already had contacted the local social service agency. The staff there was in touch with families willing to adopt children who'd been left homeless by the war. He was sure someone would be willing to take me in, someone who could give me a good home, who would see to my education and care for me. In fact, people at the agency already had one or two possibilities in mind. But it would take a little time. We would all spend the night at the station, and the next day the social workers would come to interview us.

That night at the station I slept in a real bed for the first time in four years.

Early the next day two social workers arrived bringing along a woman who was interested in taking a child—the wife of a deputy burgomaster. She was smartly dressed with lots of makeup and jewelry, and she talked in kind of a snooty voice—not at all the sort of person any of us would be drawn to. We were all introduced to her, but she mostly addressed her attentions to me and I felt rather proud when I heard her whisper to one of the agents, "I'll take the little blonde girl."

A wild, unmannered street urchin, I felt awkward in the company of this fancy lady. I didn't know how to behave or what to say to her, so when Officer Martens offered to drive us to her house I was relieved at the prospect of having company along. I quickly jumped in the front seat with him, and the lady—I forget her name—sat in the back. As we were driving along she began telling us about her house and her husband, and I heard her say, "Of course there wouldn't be a bed for her, but we have a nice big sofa.."

This fine lady was offering not a bed but a sofa! After all this, a sofa! All I could think was that I was going to be a servant again with another Madame DeWael. I wanted to jump out of the moving car and run. Officer Martens, bless him, must have seen the look on my face.

"Well, Madame, perhaps it wouldn't be right to put you out..."

"Oh, no, Monsieur, it's perfectly fine. It's just, you understand, that..."

"Madame," he continued, "I was going to mention that there are two unmarried sisters, two teachers, who very much want to have this child, and they can give her a room with a bed. I shall phone them as soon as we return to the station. It would undoubtedly be best for all concerned."

He dropped the burgomaster's wife at her door, then reversed direction and headed back to the station to call the sisters.

When we returned to the police station, the surprise of my life was waiting for me. I couldn't believe my eyes. Finally! Finally! Something good happened to me! There, in the flesh, stood Grandfather! His white hair had thinned a bit, his face was more lined than before, he'd put on a little weight and he seemed to be leaning harder on his cane, but he was unmistakably Grandfather. I raced to his arms, tears of joy pouring down my cheeks, and we hugged each other tightly and kissed many times, both of us overcome with emotion.

Then the questions poured out of me. What happened to the farm? Where was he living now? How did he know how to find me? Would Marthe be coming? I had a million of them. But after so much time, I felt awkward asking one big question: Could I live with them now?

Grandfather had some sad news: Marthe had become very sick and died. He had been obliged to sell the farm and was living in an apartment not far from the police station. He worked part-time in the town hall and the authorities always informed him when a batch of homeless children was brought in. As soon as he heard of the latest group he contacted the social service agency and the police.

The old man had trouble standing for long. Leaning hard on his cane, he led me over to a wooden bench in the corner and we sat down. Then he gave me the answer to my unspoken question.

"*Petite*, I wanted you to come and live with me, but they won't allow it."

"Won't allow it! But why? It would be so wonderful. I'd take care of you, you'd take care of me…"

"No. They told me that an old man like me couldn't properly care for you."

"But I don't understand… that's crazy!"

"It is crazy. But there's nothing I can do."

Then Grandfather told me something I already knew: that two women teachers were interested in taking me and could make me a good home.

Of course I was not pleased. What sort of an alternative was that to living with Grandfather? The old man tried hard to reassure me. He said he'd come visit me often as soon as I was settled in with the teachers. He too wanted to meet them. He would stay with me at the police station until they arrived.

We waited on the bench side by side, wrapped in our own thoughts, feeling joy and disappointment at the same time. Then during a long silence I saw him look at me with deep sadness in his eyes and I suddenly knew the answer to the most pressing question of all, the one that never had ceased to obsess me: Where were my parents?

They were gone, I could see it in his eyes. Sooner or later I would have to absorb the truth, admit it to myself. Officially, that day, I became an orphan of the war.

I sat there trying to think and wanting not to think at the same time, but the hole in my heart was so painful I couldn't hold back the tears. Quietly Grandfather drew my arm through his and began to speak reassuringly to me: I had to remember that he was with me, that he would come to visit me often, he promised, and I could visit him and someday—who could tell?—maybe he and I would be together.

The station door opened and Grandfather and I looked up at the same time. Two women, both wearing neat little hats and dark suits, stood in the entrance looking around for the proper official to address. From behind the desk I heard Office Martens' voice:

"Ah, good afternoon, ladies! Thank you for coming so promptly. The little girl is right over here."

As the women approached, Grandfather slowly raised

himself up on his cane, put his hand on my shoulder, squeezing it hard as if to transfer all his strength to me, and whispered, "Your new life, *petite*."

EPILOG

MY WILD EXISTENCE CAME TO AN ABRUPT HALT when the war ended, but my life did go on, a completely different adventure.

I never discovered what happened to my parents—who took them, where they went, how they died. Grandfather told me he believed they had been betrayed, but he could provide me with little concrete information about them or my life before he met me. A kind-hearted man who wanted to help a child in distress, he had met my mother only once and it was understood in those times that one did not ask questions. He was, therefore, unable to fill in any details of my early childhood.

Soon after we were reunited, Grandfather gave me the envelope that Leopold had handed him during my first visit to the farm. It contained the photographs taken of me at the Polyphoto shop in my new identity as "Monique DeWael." I learned that it was he who had chosen my new name, "Monique," from the Greek word "monos," meaning "alone." He also gave me some treasured photographs of himself, Marthe and me, several of which have been included in this book.

I lived with the spinster school teachers for about two years and resumed my education. What I needed to know was not only in books; I had to learn to live in society. By observation, I learned how to express and defend myself with the tools and weapons of humans—words. I attended Mass and wore dowdy old maiden's clothes, just like theirs, that I hated with a teenager's passion. Despite their best efforts to turn me into a good Catholic girl, I remained a wild creature, full of anger and challenge, who would actually bite when distressed.

While living with the sisters I went to town hall to try to find some information about my parents. Naturally, with almost no clues, there was nothing to be learned there. When they found out what I'd done, the sisters became upset, calling me ungrateful and foolish for digging up the past. I also attempted to write down all the things that had happened to me, but when they read my story they were angry and accused me of making it all up. I remember standing by the fireplace watching my journal go up in flames, page by page. Decades would pass before I attempted to tell my story again.

I studied to become a teacher, not by my own choice, but because of the sisters' enthusiasm for their profession. On the day I received my diploma I met a psychology instructor in the hall who asked,

"What are you going to do now?"

"I'll go to America."

"Do you know anyone there?"

"No."

"Do you want to go to Africa? I know of a good job. It pays well."

"Okay."

"Don't you want to think about it?"

"It's all thought out!"

Five days later I was on a boat on my way to Africa. For the next two years I lived and worked on that passenger boat, looking after children of passengers and traveling between Brussels and the Belgian Congo (now Zaire.) When the political situation there began to deteriorate, I quit my job—I had no desire to be in the middle of another war.

Back in Brussels and unemployed, I arrived for an interview with the personnel director of a "temp" agency and was astonished to see behind the desk a woman with flaxen hair and pale eyes whom I immediately recognized as Liane. Though my papers were not in order, she gave me a job when I showed her a photo of my dog. "That's papers enough," she said laughing.

Soon after, Grandfather and I finally had an opportunity to live together for one year, until he passed away and I was alone again.

Unlike people, old habits do not die quickly. For many years I did not reveal that I am Jewish or anything about my past. But in other ways the changes I noticed in myself were unexpected and, at first, surprising. Back in civilization, my body began to react as it never had when I was in the wild: I developed illnesses. In winter, I was cold all the time. I ate voraciously, wolfing down huge portions of food at a sitting.

Frantically I stocked up on anything and everything, filling cupboards to overflowing. I had a passion for beautiful clothes. I, who had marched with rags around my feet, filled closets to the ceiling with shoes. I who had nothing, bought and bought, just to possess. All the while I knew that I was not like other people. How could I not be alone among others, different and strange, after all those years in exile?

My circumstances changed when, one day in December 1985, with my husband, my son and all my pets, I crossed the ocean and disembarked in my new country. Here in America I finally would have the opportunity, and feel distant enough, to tell my story.

After a while here it became important to me to reconnect with my past, and so I joined a temple, though I have been non-religious for most of my life. Someone in the congregation learned that I had lived in Europe during the Holocaust and I was asked to tell about my experiences. My old mistrust made me hesitate; for me; to interact with people is to take off my bullet-proof vest. Yet after all those years of silence, somehow I managed to speak.

How did I endure all those terrible things? As I've told my story here, remembering and reliving all the horror and injustice, I've had nightmares again. But looking back, I can see the positive forces at work that enabled me to survive. Certainly, these three were all crucial: hope that I someday would find my parents, luck in amazing quantities and the will to live despite all suffering. And one more, my freedom. Only those who have lost their liberty understand what a blessing that was. The truth is, when it comes to survival, given the right set of circumstance we are all capable of anything. Only when we come face to face with death do we learn what unimaginable feats, heroic or vile, we may perform.

Could the Holocaust happen again? people often ask me. My answer: It has happened again. At any time, somewhere in the world, it is happening right now. An evil on the enormous scale of the Holocaust could not have been perpetrated by a small handful of deranged fiends, individuals wholly different from ourselves. By the hundreds of thousands, even by the millions, ordinary people had to compromise, collude and acquiesce. The Holocaust is not over now—nor will it ever be.

On the outside my life looks normal today, but some wounds will never heal. It is hard to believe in love when one has witnessed what I have, to forget the so-called "normal" people who chose to be blind so they wouldn't see the woes of their neighbors, to be deaf so they wouldn't hear their cries. Sometimes my sorrow and rage are as strong as when they first took root within me. At other times I feel I have been given two missions—to bear witness and to help animals as they helped me. I am still different, an animal in a human body. I find my serenity in nature, and I find God in whatever is beautiful and good.

This book is a memoir of a particular period of my life. Half a century later, I cast back the net of memory and drew up what I could. I am not a historian; the names, places, dates and incidents are as real as I can remember or reconstruct them from whisps and fragments. My story is a stone I drop into the lake, never knowing where the ripples will reach.

From those who read this, I ask compassion for all living things. And I wish you peace.